I0720786

Come Back to Me
(Stay With Me #2)

A Novel

By Carolyn Astfalk

Full Quiver Publishing

Pakenham ON Canada

This book is a work of fiction.
Characters and incidents are products of the author's
imagination.

Come Back to Me
Copyright 2020 Carolyn Astfalk

Published by
Full Quiver Publishing
PO Box 244
Pakenham, Ontario K0A 2X0
www.fullquiverpublishing.com

ISBN Number: 978-1-987970-13-5
Printed and bound in the USA
Cover design: James Hrkach, Carolyn Astfalk
Image credit: Banana Oil, Shutterstock

NATIONAL LIBRARY OF CANADA
CATALOGUING IN PUBLICATION

ALL RIGHTS RESERVED
No part of this publication may be reproduced, stored in a
retrieval system or transmitted, in any form or by any means —
electronic, mechanical, photocopying, recording or otherwise —
without prior written permission from the author.

Published by FQ Publishing
A Division of Innate Productions

*For my parents, Peter and Marcella,
my first and best example of an enduring marriage.*

1

Stay or Leave

November

By age twenty-nine, Alan Reynolds's shin had been bruised by a baseball bat, his lip split by a fist, and his ribs kicked with a steel-toed boot. Jenny Snavely spat on him in the fifth grade. When he was fourteen, his brother, Chris, kneed him in the crotch so hard he'd puked. He'd never been slapped nor had a door slammed in his face.

Until now.

He jerked backward as the door swung shut and a rush of air blew the blond wisps of hair hanging over his eye. He pounded on the door with his fist. "C'mon, Jamie. This is ridiculous."

What had gotten into his wife? She'd been edgy and emotional for weeks, crying over nothing and lashing out over inconsequential stuff. Ten minutes ago, they'd been making love, and now he stood on their stoop in nothing but unlaced sneakers and a pair of unbuttoned cargo shorts, locked out of his house.

He pounded again. "Jamie!"

A car motor hummed in the neighbor's driveway. The engine quieted, and Mrs. Simpson, his friendly neighbor who unfortunately considered herself a friend of his mother's, emerged from her silver Toyota.

Don't look my way. Don't look my way. Don't look my way.

She looked his way, cocking an eyebrow.

Alan lifted a hand in a half-hearted wave as a chilly breeze ruffled his hair and raised goose bumps on his arms.

Mrs. Simpson gave him a twitchy smile, waved, and then ambled to the front door, gawking at him as she fit her key in the lock.

He crossed his arms over his bare chest and tried to cover his exposed skin. Heat rose in his cheeks and neck as he shifted his weight from one foot to the other. November in South Central Pennsylvania was not the time or place to be shirtless.

He crossed his arms in front of him to ward off the chill sending a shiver up his neck. If he got hypothermia, it would be Jamie's fault. He lifted his hand to knock again when the door swung open. Good. Maybe now he could talk some sense—

Jamie's arm darted out the door, and his tan duffel bag thudded on the concrete at his feet. In the time it took for him to survey the bag, she'd retreated and slammed the door.

He growled and pounded again. "Jamie? A shirt, at least? Please?" He sunk his hands into his pockets and waited. Maybe she'd stuffed one in the bag?

A second later, the door opened several inches and his balled-up "Drinks Well With Others" t-shirt sailed out and into the barren flower bed.

He let out a breath, blowing his wispy bangs into the air, then snatched his shirt from the mulch. He shook out the dirt, but not the wrinkles, and pulled it over his head. Hoisting the duffel bag on his shoulder, he stomped to the red Mazda Miata.

Good thing he'd left the keys in there. Another thing that drove Jamie crazy. He turned the key in the ignition and sat half a minute, wondering where he should go. No sense checking into a hotel. Jamie would probably change her mind and beg him to come home before dark. She would, wouldn't she?

He could try his buddy Nick, but he'd met someone at the bar last night and was probably still holed up with her in his apartment. He could go to his parents' place, but Mom would give him the third degree, and Dad would give him that "I'm disappointed in you" look that made him feel like he was ten again and had gotten caught climbing the neighbors' fence to skinny dip in their pool.

He glanced at the dashboard clock. Almost noon. Chris and Rebecca should be home from church by now. The whole city could be in a state of emergency, and their bottoms would still be parked in a pew Sunday morning. According to the current zeitgeist, that should make them judgy and intolerant, but they'd only ever met Alan, a perpetual heathen, with kindness and empathy—at least so far.

He searched for something to do, someplace to go. Nothing came to mind. He sighed and backed out of the driveway. Sponging off his little brother wounded his pride, but he'd go.

For the second time in a half hour, Alan stood on a stoop pounding repeatedly on a door. At least this time he had on a shirt. And expected a better welcome.

The door opened, and his sister-in-law, Rebecca, stepped into the entranceway. Her long, wavy brown hair hung loosely over her shoulders as if she hadn't combed it yet. Her eyes and cheeks glowed as she smiled. At least someone was glad to see him.

A tight t-shirt hugged her breasts, which had grown increasingly larger as of late. His gaze snagged on her abdomen, and he sucked in a breath. He hadn't seen her in a few weeks. She was finally showing, her belly rounded where his little niece or nephew lived and grew.

This was a bad idea.

"Alan, c'mon in. This is a surprise." Her voice was louder than usual, and she flicked a glance behind her as if searching for someone. His brother, Chris, presumably.

"Thanks." He crossed the threshold and dropped his bag in the entranceway.

She darted a glance at the bag and then slung an arm around his shoulder and planted a kiss on his cheek. "Good to see you." Her hair smelled like his brother's aftershave, all woodsy and spicy, not delicate and feminine.

He lifted his chin in acknowledgment, but wondered if she'd be so glad when she knew he might be staying. "Chris around?"

She closed the door behind him. "Yeah, he's—"

Chris strode into the room in a pair of gym shorts, pulling an undershirt over his head.

Rebecca's cheeks pinked.

"Alan? What's up?" He tugged the shirt down to his waist.

Shoot. Here he'd thought they'd be getting settled after church. His gaze darted between the two of them. Yep, he'd interrupted something all right. "Listen, if this is a bad time, I can—"

"Don't be silly." Rebecca walked ahead of him toward the kitchen. "Want a cup of coffee?"

He studied Chris's face expecting a "Get your keister outta here" look, but found nothing but contentment.

Alan followed Rebecca, but when he reached Chris he whispered, "I can go. I'm pretty sure you were—"

Chris shook his head and squeezed Alan's shoulder. "No worries. We'll pick it up later." He winked.

"I thought you said she was sick." Chris had told him Rebecca had been lying around half-sick, half-asleep, gagging down saltines since a couple weeks after they learned she was pregnant.

"Second trimester." Chris dropped his arm, shrugged, and grinned. "She says her, uh, renewed interest in me is normal."

Would Jamie have been after him like that if she'd gotten pregnant? No use wondering. That was a dead end.

A laptop sat open on the kitchen table next to a large blue mug. Catalog images of baby stuff filled the screen. Glider chairs, infant swings, swaddling blankets.

He rubbed a hand across his forehead. He should've gone to his parents' place. He didn't want them to know the state of his marriage, but staying here would be like reliving that kick to the crotch Chris had delivered fifteen years ago.

Rebecca giggled as Chris stood behind her at the kitchen counter and whispered in her ear. Her arm wound around him, playing with the hair at the nape of his neck.

What possessed him to think bunking in the love shack would be a fitting refuge from his disintegrating marriage?

Rebecca disentangled herself from Chris and held up an empty mug. "Coffee, Alan?"

"Yeah. Sure. Thanks." He pulled out a wooden chair and sat opposite the open laptop. White cupboards made the small kitchen seem larger. Like the rest of the house, it was decorated neatly but simply. A narrow bookcase sat against the rear wall next to the back door. He'd helped Chris build it to store Rebecca's cookbooks. The countertops were clear except for a large stand mixer. His sister-in-law probably used the space for baking. Not like Jamie. Their remodeled kitchen remained a mere showpiece. He couldn't remember the last time the oven had been used.

They'd bought the oven a couple of months before the wedding, when Jamie had decided the old—but functional—avocado-colored model wouldn't suit the kitchen update they'd paid a handyman to do.

"How much will you take for the floor model with the dent?" Alan had pinned the Wilford Brimley lookalike wearing a red hardware apron with his best closing-the-deal stare. Why pay top dollar for an appliance whose exclusive use would be reheating leftovers and takeout?

Jamie huffed and elbowed him in the ribs. "Don't you care about *anything*? I could buy a twenty-dollar camp stove, plop it on the deck, and you'd be fine with it!"

No argument there. "What's the point of spending an arm and a leg on some double oven, self-cleaning model when we eat at restaurants or get takeout six nights a week?"

Just another thing they'd been at odds about.

Rebecca slid a mug of coffee in front of him and sat next to Chris. She sipped from a giant bottle of seltzer water.

Chris folded his hands on the table. "So, what's up? You never *just* stop by." He nodded toward the other room. "And what's with the bag?"

"Yeah. Sorry about that. I, uh . . ." Being humbled in front of his younger brother just wasn't right. He'd been with more girls than he could count before he'd married Jamie. Meanwhile, Chris had lived like a monk. Alan wasn't supposed to be the one with woman trouble, Chris was.

He rubbed a hand across his forehead. "Jamie sorta kicked me out."

Chris reclined and blew out a breath, the wooden chair groaning under his weight.

Rebecca reached across the table for his hand, pity in her eyes. "Oh, Alan. I'm so sorry."

With an arm around Rebecca's chair, Chris leaned forward. "What happened?"

"I don't know. One minute we were, uh, in bed, and then

. . ." Through a break in the clouds, sunlight had streamed in the window, giving Jamie's soft, fair skin a veritable glow. Love for her swelled in his chest as he ran his fingers across her neck and along her shoulder. His gaze followed, trailing his fingers to her belly and then— "next thing I know she's tossing my duffel bag out the door after me."

"Well, something must've happened. You been having more trouble?" Chris's brow creased.

His concern touched Alan. Whatever differences they had—and they were many—they were blood.

"Yes and no." When *hadn't* he and Jamie been having trouble? "I mean, nothing new, just these last couple of months . . . it's been worse." He mulled over his words, combing through their disagreements.

A memory flashed in his mind—Jamie on her hands and knees retrieving plastic forks and red SOLO cups from beneath their deck the morning after their Halloween party, refusing to say goodbye as he readied for a paintball game with his buddies. Two concert tickets were riding on that game!

He squatted beside her, checking the time on his phone. "I'll get that tomorrow, babe."

Jamie growled, crushing another cup and tossing it into a small heap of trash beside her.

"I gotta go." But he couldn't. Not with her angry. "Hey, I said I'll get it tomorrow."

She sat back on her heels and blew out a breath. "I'm almost done. Just go."

He stood, his feet itching to move. If he didn't leave now, he'd be late. "But you're—"

"Not everything is about you, Alan."

"No, but . . ." He really needed to go. Now. "Tell me what's bothering you then and—"

"You can't *fix* everything, y'know?" She dismissed him

with a wave of her hand.

And he left.

The sound of Rebecca's chair scraping brought Alan back to attention.

She stood and smoothed a hand over her belly. "Sorry. Indigestion. It's better if I stand."

It hit him—that was the difference these last months. Rebecca's pregnancy.

Jamie and Rebecca weren't particularly close. Their interests and personalities stood in stark contrast. But they got along and seemed to respect one another. He knew Jamie harbored some hard feelings about Rebecca eliminating her best friend Megan's chances with Chris, but it wasn't personal.

Still, that's about when things in his marriage had gone south.

From the second Chris and Rebecca had walked into Mom and Dad's house, they'd been attached at the hip with stupid grins plastered to their faces. They'd exchanged a couple furtive glances, whispered into each other's ears, and then Chris blurted right over top of Mom's rambling about her herb garden: "We're having a baby!"

Even before Mom had squealed with delight, Jamie had shrunk back, inadvertently bumping Alan.

As much as Alan wanted to truly feel happy for them, a strange weight had settled on him instead. No one acknowledged it aloud, but it increased the pressure on him and Jamie to have a baby of their own.

Chris's voice, low and hesitant, broke through his thoughts. "You want to talk about it?"

No. Hadn't he already been humiliated enough showing up here? He massaged his temples with his fingertips. Chris would listen, so maybe he should. But not now. He'd just arrived. Rebecca was here. "Later, maybe?"

Rebecca capped her water bottle and set it back in the refrigerator. "I'm going to take a little nap." She ran a hand through Chris's hair and dropped a kiss onto his head.

"Okay, hon." He rose from his chair and escorted her to the hall.

He whispered to her for several seconds, and she nodded. Probably discussing what to do with Alan's sorry behind. He hated imposing on them, especially since they were still newlyweds.

He fiddled with his thumbnails a moment or two until Chris returned.

Chris sat and scooted toward the table, his chair scraping the floor. "Okay, Alan. What's up? How can we help?"

Alan waited until the bedroom door clicked shut. He had to give Chris something, especially if he was going to impose on him. "I wish I knew. I mean, we have some stuff we disagree on. Everyone does, right? But the last couple of months . . . I don't know. It's like it all fell apart. She's always moody. Some days she's just looking to pick a fight."

Chris nodded like he understood, but he didn't. He couldn't. He and his church-going, domestic, fertile new wife were over-the-moon happy and going at it like a couple of rabbits. If it were anyone but his brother, he'd be jealous.

"So what happened today? Why'd she throw you out?"

Alan took a deep breath. What *had* happened? And if part of his problem with Jamie was due to Rebecca's pregnancy, how much should he say to Chris?

"Things were okay this morning. At least I thought so. I got up before her, made us Mom's pancakes. We ate, and then we watched some stuff on Netflix. And then we . . ."

Chris raised his brows. "You what?"

"We went back to bed."

"Oh." His brow wrinkled. "Sounds like everything was fine. I don't get it."

"It was after. I asked her if she was, uh, y'know . . ." He'd planted a kiss on her belly, his heart strangely about to burst, his love for her in that moment so intense. What would it be like to pour that love out on a baby—a gurgling, chubby-cheeked result of their love? He traced a circle around her belly button with his index finger. "So, you think maybe we could've just made a baby?"

Jamie had jerked upright, bedcovers flying, nearly knocking Alan off of the bed.

"Alan?" Chris stared, urging him to continue by motioning with his hand. "Asked her what?"

"Asked her if it was the right time to get pregnant."

"Have you been trying?"

"That probably depends."

Chris squinted an eye. "On what?"

"Which one of us you ask."

2

Bartender

Megan Pettrey slid onto the red, vinyl barstool and adjusted her miniskirt. Crossing her legs at the ankle, she shook out her hair and leaned against the padded edge of the long wooden bar. The entire scene bored her, yet here she was. Again. She hadn't done "alone" well in years. Too much time to dwell on the myriad ways in which life disappointed.

She glanced to her right, where she'd already caught the attention of two guys sipping their beers. One was just okay- looking, nondescript features, super short, black hair and an indistinguishable tattoo on the inside of his forearm. His friend's frame was more muscular, his features all-American boy next door type. He leered over the edge of his mug and winked.

She averted her gaze. A little game of hard to get never hurt anyone. In fact, in her experience, it made her even more desirable. Guys wanted the hunt, the chase. To feel like they'd won a girl over. Most guys anyway. She could think of one who'd been immune to her appeal for more than a decade.

A lost cause.

The mirror behind the bar offered her a discreet means of checking out the other side of the bar as well. One man, his suit jacket draped over the back of his stool, slouched over a mixed drink. They said misery loved company, but Megan didn't love misery. She had enough of her own.

The bartender stopped, pulled a damp rag from beneath

the bar and cleaned the surface in front of her. He placed a white cocktail napkin on the bar and tapped his fingers as if he were drumming. "What can I get you, darlin'?"

She tilted her head and gave him a seductive grin. "I don't know. What do you have to offer?"

He smiled and played along, but she knew from experience he was a master at the game. Like a chameleon, his colors changed to suit his environment. Whatever would bring him the largest tip.

"Hmm. How about a strawberry daiquiri?" His eyes twinkled. "Virgin."

She bit her bottom lip. "I'm allergic to strawberries. And I'm not looking for a virgin."

Her mind flitted back to a conversation she'd had with her friend Jamie at Jamie's end-of-summer pool party more than a year ago. Jamie had come up behind her as Megan peered through the sliding glass door at Chris. Keeping his distance from the crowd bunched near the pool, he perched atop the picnic table on the deck with *her* borrowed phone to his ear.

"He is not still a virgin." Megan shook her head, her gaze fixed on Chris. "There is no way. None. Uh-uh"

Jamie shrugged. "Alan says he and Rebecca are waiting."

Her heart twisted at the mention of Rebecca's name. The thought of that goody two-shoes made her sick. But, it did bring her a small measure of satisfaction that if Megan hadn't gotten Chris into bed, no one else had either.

"Yeah. Didn't think so," the bartender said with a grin. "How about a chocolate martini?"

"Sounds good."

He scooted to the other side of the bar to mix her drink, and she glanced at the two guys again. The good-looking one's eyes still focused on her. She smiled and fiddled with the corners of her napkin. *Wait for it. Ten . . . nine . . . eight . . . seven . . .*

She'd reached two when the barstool beside her squeaked as he positioned himself next to her.

"You're way too pretty a girl to be sittin' here all by yourself." His voice reeked of overconfidence and his breath of the cheap beer that fueled it.

"I don't believe I'm by myself anymore." She angled herself on the stool so that her knees pointed in his direction. Up close, his appeal lost some of its luster. His complexion was pockmarked, and he had a gap between his front teeth that reminded her of the sunken-faced jack-o'-lantern rotting on her neighbor's stoop. Not that it mattered. If she were looking for a relationship, this pancake joint by day, dive bar by night would be the last place she'd go.

His gaze dipped to her stocking-covered thighs then slowly made its way to her eyes, snagging for an extra second on her chest.

Three martinis later, Ryan—that was his name, right?—Ryan pushed his empty glass mug toward the bartender. "I'll be right back. Don't you go anywhere."

She slid her hand up the leg of his jeans. "I'll be right here, waiting."

The bar had filled up over the last hour and a half. Only a few seats remained open. Megan drained the last of the martini from her glass and ran her turquoise-polished nail along the rim. Should she invite Ryan to her place for . . . whatever? It would probably be safer, but then he'd know where she lived.

The scent of a musky cologne drifted toward her, and someone jostled her elbow.

"Sorry," a man's voice mumbled.

She swiveled toward him. "No need to be—" Her brows rose as she recognized that blond hair and strong jaw, currently clenched with lips twisted in a frown. "Well, look what the wind blew in. What are you doing here? Isn't this a little off your well-beaten, bar-hoppin' path?"

"Megan?" Alan's blue eyes grew wide.

She leaned around him then glanced over her shoulder. "Is Chris—"

"No. I'm alone." He repositioned himself on the stool and motioned for the bartender. "And you shouldn't be asking about him. He's married. In fact, he's going to be a dad soon."

Her throat went dry. "He is?"

"Didn't Jamie tell you?"

She shook her head. Jamie hadn't told her much of anything lately. The circle of friends they'd shared had fallen apart a few months ago, and their biweekly girls' night had gone by the wayside.

"Yeah. Rebecca's four or five months pregnant." He stared at bottles of vodka lining the back of the bar, a faraway look in his eye.

She let out a scoffing laugh, sounding more bitter than she intended. "Well, I guess the little virgin Mary finally—"

He grabbed her arm and turned her toward the bar so that she no longer faced him. "Listen, I don't know what your problem is with her. It's not like you had something going with Chris. She's my sister-in-law, and if you're going to talk smack about her, I'll find somewhere else to sit."

"Touchy, touchy." She fingered her sleeve where he'd touched it. "I'll lay off Saint Rebecca."

He rolled his eyes but didn't move from the stool.

"So, is Jamie sick or something?"

"Something."

She leaned into his field of vision and wrinkled her brow. "Where *is* Jamie?"

"Like I know."

"What's that supposed to mean?"

On the rare occasions they'd texted or called lately, Jamie had been complaining more and more frequently about Alan. Said he was pressuring her to have a baby. Apparently, whatever was brewing between them had come to a head.

He cast Megan a sidelong glance, turned his gaze to the gleaming bar top, and twisted his lips. "It means your *friend* kicked me out of my own house this morning for no good reason."

"Well, what no good reason could she—" A strong arm wrapped around her shoulders, and Ryan's beer breath curled around her ear. "Hey, beautiful. What do you say we get out of here?"

She caught Alan's glare in her peripheral vision. What was his problem? She was single and unattached. She could leave the bar with anyone she chose. "Ryan, this is Alan. He's sort of a friend of the family."

Ryan sized up Alan and nodded in his direction. "Hey." He leaned into Megan. "You ready?"

"Absolutely." The word slurred as she teetered off the bar stool.

Alan's protective arm curled around her back, steadying her. She twisted and brushed it away. Who did he think he was anyway?

"You're drunk, Megan. Give the guy your number, if you want, and let me take you home."

"Hey, are we going?" Ryan sounded impatient.

She'd been about to leave with him, but his presumption perturbed her. Maybe she ought to stay. "Listen, how about I—"

"Sorry, man. I'm going to give her a lift." Alan stepped between her and Ryan. "She's in no shape to go anywhere with you."

Ryan huffed, emitting a whistle through the gap in his teeth, tossed a few bills on the bar, and stomped away.

Jerk.

The bartender finally appeared, and Alan ordered a beer.

"I'll just have one, and then I'll drop you off, okay?" He shrugged out of his jacket and draped it behind his seat.

"Uh-uh. I'll Uber." Yes, she'd lost one overprotective big brother, but she didn't need Alan trying to take his place.

"What do you mean, Uber? I'll give you a ride."

"You'll do no such thing. If it gets back to Jamie—"

"It's not going to get back to Jamie, but so what if it does? Unless she's gone completely batty, she'll be grateful I was looking out for you."

Not the Jamie she knew. Maybe Alan didn't realize it, but Jamie had a possessive, jealous streak. She recalled the string of catty remarks Jamie had whispered about the restaurant hostess who'd flirted with Alan the last time they'd been out to dinner together. "No, she'll think something's up between us."

"That's ridiculous. First of all, I'm married." He ticked off the reasons on his fingers. "You're her friend. You've always had a thing for my brother."

She shook her head. Clueless man.

He blew out a breath and pulled his cell phone from his pocket. "Okay. You win. I'm calling Tim. He'll come get you."

She grabbed his arm, nearly knocking the phone out of his hand with her lack of coordination. "No."

"What do you mean 'no'? He's your brother. He'll be here."

"No, he won't." She turned back to the bar as the

bartender slid Alan's beer toward him. "Give me another." She held up her martini glass.

"How many have you had? If you're not going to let me drive you, Tim can—"

"No. Tim's not around."

"How do you know?" He swiped at the phone, pressed some buttons, and held it up to his ear.

She swatted it away.

"Hey." Irritation rose in his voice. "Watch it!"

She sighed and leaned back into the stool. "I told you, Tim's not around." Why couldn't he let it go? Dread pitted in her stomach at the thought of explaining.

"Where is he?"

"He's gone for a month. One of those . . ." She gestured with her arm as she tried to come up with the name. "A place you dry out. . . Rehab."

His eyes widened. "What? Tim's in rehab? I-I know he liked his beer. And whiskey. But, I didn't think—"

"Yeah, well. It's stupid. Total waste of time and money. Met some girl and says he wants to—"—she made loose air quotes—"clean up his act." If what's-her-name couldn't accept Tim as he is, then she should find someone else. Maybe *she* wasn't good enough for *him*.

He shook his head. "Huh. I should've known, I guess. I mean, I'm supposed to be his friend."

"Yeah. Well, you and Jamie have both been kind of preoccupied these last few months."

"But still. I feel bad." He gulped his beer and then settled the pint glass in front of him.

The bartender set another martini in front of her, and she sipped. "Don't sweat it."

"That settles it then. I'll drive you home." He glanced at his watch and then pinned her with a stern look. "I'll finish this beer, and then we'll go."

"Whatever." If he'd rather play Uber driver than repair his marriage, that was on him.

22

3
Trouble

Alan's car rolled to a stop in front of Megan's apartment. She lived on the first floor of a three-story building, one of about fifty identical structures in the complex. A green sign pointed the direction to the walking path and the outdoor pool. Looked like a safe enough place.

He turned the engine off and surveyed his passenger. Eyes closed, head lolled to the side, shoulders slouched.

"Megan."

No response.

"Megan. We're here. C'mon." He shook her arm.

She groaned but didn't move.

"That a girl. We're here."

He exited the car, came around to her side and opened the door. His hand pressed to her arm kept her from flopping out and onto the concrete.

"Megan. Come on. I'm not carrying you." Scanning her long, slim legs exposed below her super-short skirt, her trim waist, and narrow shoulders beneath a tight blouse, he assessed her weight. He could lift her under normal circumstances, but she was going to be dead weight tonight. And though he'd dismissed her worries about Jamie thinking something was up between them, carrying an unconscious woman—not your wife—into her apartment just wasn't right. Maybe he should've called Chris, if for nothing else than to have a witness, but given Megan's history of pining after Chris . . .

Megan rubbed a hand across her forehead. "Where are we?"

"Your place. Let's go." He reached into the car, tugged her upright, then steadied her on her feet.

***

The sidewalk swayed beneath her feet, and she pressed her thumb and forefinger to her closed eyes. She blinked them open. One step . . . two . . . tilting . . . tilting.

Alan's hand clamped tight around her upper arm.

She brushed at his hand, missing entirely. "Let go. You're gonna bruise me."

"You're gonna be more than bruised if I let you fall to the ground."

His tone was gruff, short. Probably ticked that he'd insisted on taking her home in the first place.

When they reached the building door, she groped clumsily for the keys lost in the bottom of her bag. She rooted through a wad of napkins, her change purse, two tubes of lipstick, and a compact. They were in there somewhere.

Alan growled and grabbed hold of her purse. "Here, let me."

She released it, not caring whether he riffled through her stuff or not. The sooner her body hit the bed, the better.

In seconds, he'd opened both the main door and the door to her apartment. Light flooded the entryway, forcing her to squint and shift her gaze to the floor. Her heels sunk into the beige carpet, and she kicked them off in the direction of the closet. The floor wobbled again.

"Uh, this is where the chauffeur service ends." He sounded sheepish, totally unlike his overconfident self. Then again, he probably hadn't been alone in the company of a woman other than Jamie for a very long time.

She spun toward him a little too quickly and flung out an arm toward the wall for support.

Alan caught her elbow, sighing. "Okay. Point me to your

24

bedroom. I got you this far. I can at least deliver you safely to your bed. After that you're on your own."

Clearly *not* what he wanted to do. She could have a little fun with him. "Am I? What if I need help, y'know, getting undressed?"

His jaw clenched. "You can sleep in your clothes." He steered her in the direction she pointed and plunked her on the bed.

The mattress dipped, and she patted the spot next to her. "Wouldn't you rather stay here than go . . ." Go where? He'd said Jamie kicked him out, but now where was he staying? She made an uncontrolled circling motion with her hand. ". . . wherever you're crashing now?"

"Nope."

"Where *are* you staying?"

"None of your business." Standing legs apart and arms akimbo, he glanced around the room as if he were looking for something. He exited the room, calling over his shoulder. "I'll get you a glass of water."

She toppled back onto the bed and shut her eyes, breathing deeply and willing the room to stop spinning. She should've let what's-his-name bring her home. He would've been more fun. She'd always thought that Alan was fun. Not tonight. A total stick-in-the-mud. She slid the phone from her skirt pocket and jabbed at the screen until she'd pulled up the camera app. Her eyes slid closed again, but she clutched the phone. Alan had been nothing tonight but a pain in her—

The sound of a glass landing on her nightstand forced her eyelids open.

Alan lifted her stocking feet, forcing her back onto the bed. A little light seeped in from the entryway, casting his face in shadows. In the dark, the curve of his jaw, the set of his eyes, even the color of his hair, resembled Chris.

Chris. The mere thought of him made her pulse race, her breath quicken. How hadn't she seen the resemblance before? Maybe because their personalities were as different as Chardonnay and champagne. Chris was all quiet strength, masculinity, and sex appeal. Alan was loud bravado, machismo, and, okay, sex appeal too, but not in a way that had ever appealed to Megan. Until now.

She swung an unsteady arm around his neck, pulling him down with her. In this light, with the vodka in her bloodstream—and whatever else was in three or four chocolate martinis—she could almost imagine he *was* Chris. "Stay." Her plea came out a husky whisper.

He ducked out from under her arm, and she fell back onto the bed.

"What's with you, Megan? I don't care how much you had to drink. I'm married. To one of your best friends." His expression twisted, and he spat the last word at her, the fricative casting a spray on her forearm.

She whipped the phone upward and clicked, capturing only his forehead and her white drywall ceiling as he stepped back. *Darn. Useless shot.*

He muttered something she couldn't make out before he disappeared around the corner and the door slammed behind him.

A giggle escaped her lips followed by a hiccup so violent it shook her whole diaphragm, and she feared she might vomit. Megan breathed deeply, closed her eyes, and filled her imagination with thoughts of Chris.

***

Alan stared through the windshield at Chris and Rebecca's house. It suited them. Nothing pretentious. Sturdy brick, neat and tidy. Several pumpkins and gourds sat on the concrete steps. A wreath decorated with mini ears of Indian corn hung from the door. Nice neighborhood too. A mixture of elderly couples and young families with little kids.

He sniffed the lapel of his black wool jacket and caught a whiff of Megan's sweet perfume. Maybe it was good he wasn't going home to Jamie tonight after all. He pushed open the car door and trudged toward the house. He hoped they hadn't waited up for him. From the looks of the place, they hadn't. No light shone from the windows. Shades were drawn in the bedrooms visible from the front. He'd gone out mostly to give them some time to themselves. They hadn't exactly planned on a houseguest for the night.

As he climbed the steps to the front stoop, he checked his phone for the umpteenth time. No messages from Jamie. How many nights would it be until she took him back? Or until she at least explained why she'd tossed him out?

He inserted the house key Chris had given him and stepped into the dark entryway. A nightlight shone from the kitchen, but otherwise, darkness shrouded the rooms.

Being careful not to make any noise, he padded down the hallway to the spare bedroom and the airbed he'd inflated earlier. Eventually, this would be a children's bedroom, but for now it sat empty, save for an open box of books and a floor lamp in the corner. From the fresh-paint odor, he'd guess they'd repainted the cream-colored walls, but gouges and scratches still marked the dull hardwood floor.

After laying his coat and shoes on the floor, he fished through his pants pockets. At home, he'd toss his phone, keys, loose change, and wallet on the dining room buffet. Here, there was no place to go with them but the floor. He grabbed the toothbrush he'd picked up at drug store on his way back from Megan's and strolled to the bathroom.

Once he'd brushed his teeth, he stripped down to his shorts, pulled on an undershirt, and climbed onto the airbed, which provided a surprisingly firm cushion. Not like his bed at home, high-density foam with a half dozen other marketing gimmicks, but comfortable. He lay back and closed his eyes. Was Jamie asleep, sprawled diagonally across the bed the way she was wont to do? He rubbed a hand over his brow. No matter how tired he was, sleep would be elusive.

A muffled giggle came through the wall behind him, followed by the rumble of a deep chuckle. The mattress creaked, the bed frame groaned, and then the soft murmurs of conversation continued. Which would be worse—listening to the intimate murmurs of contented conversation or the sounds of them making love? The thought of the former made his heart ache and the latter twisted his stomach in knots.

He raised a fist to knock, to let them know their walls may not be as soundproof as they thought. With his knuckles a fraction of an inch away, he stopped, picturing Rebecca's wide, innocent brown eyes and crimson cheeks. He didn't want to embarrass her. It was their house, after all, they'd been married less than six months, and he'd already interrupted them once today.

Alan retracted his hand and stretched over the side of the airbed until he reached his phone and earbuds. He'd listen to the Dave Matthews Band until he fell asleep.

4
Can't Stop

The chorus of a derivative pop song played on a loop from Megan's phone. Groaning, she rolled onto her belly and smacked her hand against the nightstand in an attempt to make the noise stop.

Finally getting hold of the device, she swiped across the bottom and held it to her ear. "Hello?" She should've checked to see who it was. If it were Alan checking up on her—

"Megan? You sound like crap."

Tim. Sounding surprisingly not like crap for the first time in longer than she could remember.

She pushed herself up on the bed, noticing the runs in both legs of her stockings. With a hard swallow, she tried to moisten her parched throat. "Never mind me. I didn't think I'd hear from you until, y'know, you were done." Sober? Clean? As stiff and dull as a concrete pillar?

"I can make calls. Just trying to clear my head, y'know. Focus on why I'm here. But I missed you."

"Missed me, huh?" She slid off the bed and sauntered to the kitchen, the brightly colored cover of the magazine on the end table catching her eye. Where had Alan put her purse? "More like wanted to check up on me."

Tim laughed, a genuine, hearty laugh. He sounded free and happy.

Her heart burned with jealousy.

"Maybe. So, what'd you do last night?"

She opened the fridge, pushed aside a six-pack of yogurts

and the remains of a convenience store fruit smoothie, and removed a half-gallon pitcher of water. "What do you think? Went out. Had a few drinks—"

"A few?"

"More or less." She grabbed a glass from the cupboard, searching her fuzzy brain for ways to change the subject. "Ran into your buddy Alan last night."

"Oh yeah? I feel bad I didn't talk to him before I left. How's he doing?"

She filled her glass and sipped. Two glasses of water, some black coffee, and she'd be set. "Uh, apparently Jamie kicked him out."

"Aw, man. I'm sorry to hear that. I knew they'd been struggling lately, but still . . ."

"Well, I guess he's not the perfect husband his brother apparently is, and—"

"Let it go, will you, Meg?" Irritation sounded in his voice. Or maybe exasperation. "What's it going to take for you to just put Chris out of your mind? He never showed any interest, and now he's married. I mean—"

"Knocked up his wife already too, or didn't you know? Apparently, she—"

"Just don't, Megan. The envy, the meanness. It's not becoming."

Her dramatic eye roll would be lost on him over the phone.

"So, you hungover this morning?"

She popped a dark roast cup into her coffee maker and pushed the flashing blue button. Hungover? She didn't throw up anymore. Her head seldom hurt. She tried to recall the evening. Alan bringing her home was a little fuzzy. She remembered pulling—Chris?—onto the bed with her, but that couldn't be. She hadn't kissed Alan, had she? She'd messed with him, sure, but she'd never do that to

Jamie. "I'm fine. Just having a cup of coffee, ready to start the day."

Silence.

"You're a beautiful girl, Meg. You've got so much to offer a guy. And I know we've had a lot of . . ."

"Stuff?"

He chuckled.   "Yeah. Stuff to deal with, but you've gotta . . ."

Here it comes.

"You've gotta make some changes. I know you don't drink as much or as often as I did, but that doesn't mean your binge drinking isn't a problem."

Tears stung her eyes. Had she become a walking cliché, drowning her sorrows in flavored martinis and happy hour hookups?

"Megan?"

She swiped tears from her cheeks. When had her life become such a pathetic mess? That was the million-dollar question. The one she'd avoided asking. Asking meant answering, and she wasn't ready for that. "I'm here." She tried for cool and collected, but she doubted she could fool Tim.

Tim, the sometimes dismissive, sometimes sweet, older brother who'd secretly sent her candy canes in middle school so she wouldn't be left out. The brother who'd taken the place of her junior prom date when he'd bailed halfway through the evening.

"I don't mean to bust your chops. It's just, well, it's not like we were angels before."

She laughed. No, none of the Pettreys were on the fast track for sainthood. An image of Rebecca flashed in her mind, and her lip curled.

"This whole thing has forced me to take a hard look at my life. I've been wasting time. Drinking too much, yeah, but other stuff, too. Trying to control everything and getting teed off when things didn't go the way I wanted them to." He sighed then spoke softly, tenderly. "You can't tell me it's been much different for you . . . since Randy."

Her chest tightened. That place must've gotten to him. He never, *never* spoke about their older brother, Randy, gone five years now after his helicopter was shot down in Afghanistan. No one did. Not her parents, not Tim. They'd lost touch with Randy's fiancée within a couple months of the funeral.

"What about all the alcohol, Megan? And acting like you don't care, hanging onto this thing for Chris Reynolds?"

He should've left Chris out of this.

She retrieved her coffee from the machine and sipped. "I plead the fifth." No use trying to fake Tim out; he could see straight through her.

"Think about it, will you? About making some changes. You know I'm behind you a thousand percent."

She set the coffee on the counter, staring absently at the swirls of steam rising above the rim. "Okay, yeah. I'll think about it." *Later.*

5
Where Are You Going?

One good thing about staying at Chris and Rebecca's—the distance between their home and Alan's office couldn't be more than ten minutes. Close enough for him to swing by their house and grab the phone charger he'd left behind. And if he was lucky, some lunch.

Alan pulled in the driveway, killed the engine, and trotted up the concrete steps. His mouth watered as he imagined Rebecca pulling some home-baked treat from the oven. Maybe banana bread or those chocolate peanut butter bar things that he loved. What else did she have to do anyway? She'd quit her job for some kind of part-time pastry school thing at the community college that only amounted to a couple of evening classes a week and some Saturdays.

He let himself in, breathing deeply in anticipation of the rich, warm aroma. Rebecca's voice filtered in from the kitchen along with the sound of metal on ceramic. A familiar voice came over the speakerphone, and his foot froze halfway across the welcome mat.

"But Chris pursued you. More than once. He proposed to you, down on one knee with a ring." He loved Jamie's voice. Always a little rough, like she'd thrown back a shot of Janis Joplin potion. When she wanted to sound seductive, and spoke the right words, it buckled his knees. But when anger drove her, it scratched and scraped, abrasive and capable of slashing his heart to ribbons. This afternoon it neither seduced nor abraded. Her tone with Rebecca was plaintive and tinged with sadness.

Jamie must've been on her lunch hour. Did she and Rebecca talk on the phone often? He didn't think they spoke outside of family gatherings, but maybe he was wrong.

"One of you must've proposed, you're married." More clatter of metal over Rebecca's voice. Spoons maybe? She *was* baking.

He stepped backward and out the door, closing it behind him without making a sound. Forget the charger; he'd grab lunch at a fast-food drive-thru. He didn't need to hear Jamie's answer to know what she'd say next.

He hadn't even asked Jamie on a date. After four weeks of hanging out at a mutual friend's house for *Monday Night Football*, they'd become a couple. When his lease ran out at his apartment, they moved his stuff into her place with little discussion or forethought to the implications. Their decision to marry—if you could call it that—wasn't much different.

Her co-worker's Valentine's wedding reception had stretched into the wee hours of the morning. Jamie had stumbled through the hotel room door ahead of him, giggling at nothing.

He'd followed, falling against the closed door and bolting it shut. His eyes sunk closed with exhaustion as the buzz he'd had going wore off.

With ice-cold fingers, Jamie grabbed his hands and tugged him toward the king-size bed, where he flopped onto his back. She'd flicked on the light, giggling some more.

Shielding his eyes from the glare, he groaned. "What's so funny?"

"No flippin' idea." She kicked off her high heels and tucked herself against him atop the bed, nestling her head under his arm, cheek to chest. "I loved her gown. And the way they decorated the ballroom with the gold ribbons and . . ." She waved a hand in the air. "All the glittery stuff. Like a fairy tale come to life." She sighed, the alcohol on her breath overpowering the waning strength of her perfume.

He squeezed her closer, remembering the feel of her body wrapped in his arms as they'd danced earlier, conscious that they had both a giant bed and a Jacuzzi for the night. "Is that important to you?"

"What?"

"Y'know. A wedding. The white dress and the flowers and the big party." Personally, he couldn't care less, but her comments made him wonder if it was important to her. And his mom . . . it would get her off his back. He'd had enough of her not-so-subtle hints about tying the knot.

She shrugged against him, then with fumbling fingers began unbuttoning his dress shirt. "I guess. I mean, I didn't really think so. Things are fine the way they are. We don't need a piece of paper to define our relationship, but . . . maybe." She gave up on the buttons and scooted upward, propping her elbows on his chest, her eyes a little glassy but warm and loving. Her hair, tousled but still shiny, spilled over her shoulders.

He gazed at her over his chest. He liked seeing her happy and wanted to keep her that way. They had fun together. She got him in a way no other woman or girl ever had. "Let's do it then."

"Do it?"

"Yeah. Get married."

Jamie giggled again. "O-kay." Her head fell against his chest, and she worked at the buttons again. "So, like, are we engaged now?"

Engaged. That's what getting married implied, right? So . . . "Yeah, I mean, yeah . . . I guess. We're engaged." His mind spun as he attempted to process the enormity of what he'd just committed himself to. "You'll need a ring. We can get a ring. I should have a bonus coming at the end of the quarter. As long as no one cancels a contract on me."

She'd successfully negotiated all of his buttons. Except for one, which popped off and rolled onto the bed as she tugged open the shirt. "Whoops. Sorry."

He grinned, loving her easygoing way. No pressure. No demands. He could do this for the rest of his life.

Now, as he jogged down the steps toward his car, he wondered if he could or if he'd even be given the opportunity to try. Sure, he'd kind of fallen into marriage, but if the ache in his chest was any indication, it had been the best indecision of his life.

6

Crush

Golden leaves whirled like a dervish in the breeze, suddenly drifting and dropping to skitter across the two-lane road. The setting sun peeked from behind mammoth, gray clouds that pressed heavily on the horizon.

Megan braked as she approached the two-story home on her right. Leaves littered the front yard. A couple of pumpkins stood sentry on either side of the front door and light shone through one of the front windows from somewhere deep within the house.

Though not the fastest or most direct path between home and work, she'd adopted this route several years ago. All because of this house. Or rather, because of who used to live in it.

Her eyes flicked between the empty road in front of her and the room in the upper left of the house. Dark, as usual. Rarely did she spy anyone outside the home. A couple times over the past year she'd glimpsed Chris, but not once since he'd married. Apparently, his parents rattled around in the big house by themselves now. Even Alan's vehicle hadn't been spotted in the driveway for weeks.

A horn blared, startling her and bringing her attention back to the road. A white pickup truck swerved onto the opposite berm as she twisted the wheel of her black MINI Cooper, directing the vehicle onto her side of the double yellow lines. Her heart pounded in her chest as she righted the wheel.

What drew her to this house, to this man whom she'd

obsessed over for a decade? A guy who, though unfailingly polite, had never expressed any interest beyond friendship with her. Barely friendship. More like a long-term friendly acquaintance.

Megan sighed. She'd been so sure once that she could draw his interest. She could compete with other girls. She could out-flirt, out-maneuver, and out-wit any high school girl. But her competition for Chris had never been another girl. It had been music and books and, above all, his infernal shyness.

She'd been fourteen, a freshman, the first time Chris had caught her eye. Sure, she'd known him for years, but she'd never given the reserved, average-looking boy a second glance.

Her parents had argued, about what she couldn't recall. Voices raised, doors slammed, and suddenly Tim, under duress, dragged his little sister along for whatever Friday night shenanigans he had planned with his friends.

Her initial giddiness at attending a house party with a bunch of cute senior boys faded to boredom as Tim pulled up to the Reynolds' manse and lectured her on leaving him and his friends alone. He strode toward the door, his pace not allowing for her shorter stride. His tune didn't change once they got inside.

"Stay. Out. Of my business." Tim glanced around the spacious family room to which Alan had directed them. "Sit over there. On the couch." He jerked his chin toward a beige sectional sofa littered with blue plaid throw pillows. "You brought a book or something, didn't you?"

She gave him the eye roll usually reserved for their mom. "Uh, no. I thought I'd be hanging out with you."

He snorted. "No way." Tim plucked a magazine from the end table and tossed it at her. "We'll be downstairs."

Megan flipped through the stupid sports rag twice, then

stood and perused the room, checking out the framed family pictures on the wall, the country-décor knickknacks on the shelf, and the view into the sprawling, sloped backyard bathed in moonlight.

Chris slipped around the corner into the room, grinding to a halt at the sight of her. In less than a second, his cheeks reddened, and his gaze drifted to the window and then down to his shoes. His parents could probably afford designer stuff, but from his shoes to his jeans and long-sleeve t-shirt, everything he wore was no-name and nondescript. Even his hair, dark brown with a hint of wave, could only be described as "short" with no discernible style.

A grin slipped at his sudden shyness. "Hey. Tim's downstairs with your brother. I'm supposed to wait here for him." She expected some reply. After all, they'd known each other since grade school.

Eventually, Chris nodded. After several more excruciating seconds, he gestured to the television in the corner stand. "I was gonna watch a movie. *King Kong*. The re-make."

"Sounds good to me."

The next three hours passed in verbal silence. Only the sounds of the movie and an occasional burst of shouts or laughter from downstairs filled the air. Seated at opposite ends of the couch, she'd almost forgotten he was there until he retreated to the kitchen midway through the movie and popped a bag of popcorn in the microwave. He offered her some in a large blue bowl that read "Movie Time" on the side.

Jolted to the present by blinding headlights in her rearview mirror, Megan blinked and glimpsed the old basketball hoop standing in the Reynolds' driveway behind her. She doubted many balls swished through its net these days, but now that Chris and Rebecca were having a baby, it may see use again.

In the weeks after that boring night in Chris's family room, as angry chaos and loud arguments heralded her dad's departure from their home and family, the calm, quiet, steady presence of Chris Reynolds gained appeal. Then as the awkward adolescent transformed into a strikingly good-looking young man, the appeal blossomed into teen obsession.

Despite that fact Chris didn't date or even attend school dances, sharing the same bank of lockers and an occasional class at school provided enough fuel for her fantasies. Elaborate fantasies stoked by raging hormones spilled out into a spiral-bound, pink notebook bedecked with hippie-style flower illustrations in orange and green. A series of romantic encounters filled the pages, from innocuous imaginings of slow dances at the Snowball Soirée to vivid erotic dreams of being stranded in a winter cabin together.

As Megan approached the stop sign, her cell phone rang, resounding over the car's speakers via the Bluetooth. She pressed the phone button on the steering wheel to answer. "Hello."

"Hey, it's Jamie."

The image of Alan tending to her in her drunken stupor flashed in Megan's memory. Did Jamie know? Was she angry? "What's up?"

A sigh came over the speakers. "Just hoping we could get together soon. Talk. . . I could use a friend."

Should she admit she knew or just play dumb? Her gut screamed to tell her, but that would open the door to recounting the whole embarrassing evening with Alan. And despite her stupid actions that night, she didn't want to cause more trouble in their marriage. "Do you want to get a coffee or something?" She thought of the week ahead. Crunch time at work, tense Thanksgiving meal with her family. "How about Black Friday? Some coffee shop far, far from the shopping mall."

Jamie laughed. "Sounds perfect."

Silence lingered.

A twinge of guilt and sympathy pierced Megan's heart. "Is everything . . . okay?"

"Not really. My life's a mess. But it'll still be a mess Friday, I'm sure. We can talk then."

Lights flashed behind her, and a siren blared, forcing Megan to pull to the side of the road as a fire truck passed.

"Where are you?"

She glanced in the rearview mirror to make sure no more emergency vehicles trailed the fire engine. Seeing none, she pulled back onto the road. "Uh, over by your in-laws', actually. On my way home."

"That's kind of a roundabout way to your place, isn't it?"

Megan should've made something up. Told her she was somewhere else. What had she been thinking? "You know I like the scenic route."

"Megan, seriously. You know I love you, and I would've liked to have seen you together, but he's *married*. Very happily, I might add." A note of irritation sounded in her voice. Jealousy maybe? "And he's gonna be a daddy soon too."

The mention of Rebecca's pregnancy caused an ache in Megan's chest. It wasn't worth denying she'd driven this way in hope of spotting Chris. Jamie knew her too well to buy a lie. "I heard the blessed news."

"From who? *Please* tell me you're not stalking him on trips to the obstetrician's office."

"Alan told me." Megan clamped her mouth shut. Shoot. Now Jamie would wonder when she'd seen him.

"Alan?" Her voice quavered. "You've . . . you've seen him?"

Megan scrambled for a way to extricate herself from the conversation. "Hey, it looks like there's an accident up ahead. I need to concentrate on the road. Text me about coffee on Friday, okay?"

She disconnected the call before Jamie's response even left her mouth. What was she doing? She didn't want to jeopardize her friendship with Jamie. Real friends were hard to come by. Especially girl friends. Ones that didn't judge and harp on her behavior. Ones that listened.

And what about Chris? Why did she cling to the ridiculous hope that someday her dreams of being with him would come true?

She'd invested so much in the fantasy. So much hope. So much of her heart. It had been a constant in a sea of change.

She'd even finagled her way to Alan's wedding before she and Jamie had become close. They'd become friendly not long before the wedding, and Jamie had tried to put in a good word with Chris. It hadn't worked, but the wedding . . . she thought if only she could get him alone at the wedding, share a couple of drinks, a dance . . .

But Chris had brought Rebecca and barely left her side the whole evening. He'd even kissed her on the dance floor, driving Megan back to the bar for another round.

Megan pressed her fingers into her now-achy forehead. It was past time to let go of her obsession. Past time to face the fact that she'd become what her dad had always thought she'd be: the kind of girl guys used as a plaything, not the kind they married. Not the kind guys like Chris Reynolds married. Only her dad didn't see the big picture, that as much as guys used her, she used them more.

7
Out of My Hands

Outside Chris and Rebecca's house, Alan stomped up the stairs, his hunter green suitcase bumping along behind him. As he released the handle, the suitcase teetered on the concrete and then pitched backward. He thrust his leg against it, keeping it from toppling down the steps. Hoisting his laptop bag to the other shoulder, he tucked his empty coffee cup between his elbow and chest, and then transferred his toiletries bag to the other hand. With his free hand, he fished the house key from his pocket.

The brass-colored keys dangled from a medallion doubling as a keychain. He swung the silver medallion into his palm and studied the image. Some old guy with a pointy hat and a staff. A clean-shaven Gandalf or something? Tiny words in what looked like Latin ran along the edge. The pope? *Weird.* He shook his head, grasped one of the keys and jammed it into the lock.

He twisted the knob a couple times, trying not to drop anything, then pushed the door open with his shoulder, his vinyl bag sliding to his elbow. He crushed the coffee cup into his side and tried jerking the bag back up as he grabbed hold of the rolling suitcase handle. The wheels caught on the threshold, hampering his progress so that he tumbled rather than walked into the foyer.

The cup hit the rug, and a string of curses flew from his lips as he steadied himself and jammed the luggage pull handle into the troublesome suitcase. Tension built in his neck and shoulders, and he kicked the suitcase in

43

aggravation, knocking it onto its side.

A whiff of something savory came from the kitchen, warm and garlicky and like everything that came from that kitchen, delicious. His anger subsided while his appetite grew, and he lunged for the wayward cup.

A pair of battered, brown loafers and a hand came into view, scooping up the cup, which remained out of Alan's reach. "Here you go. Good thing it was empty, huh?"

Alan's gaze darted to the man holding his crushed cup, which now had a trickle of coffee running from the rim to the paperboard holder. The man in front of him smiled, and for a fraction of a second, Alan thought him a stranger. Then he caught the quirk of his grin and the strong line of his nose. "Father John, I almost didn't recognize you." His gaze roamed over the gray sweatshirt with blue letters that read "Seminary," paired with faded blue jeans.

"Yeah." Father John glanced at his attire. "Probably never seen me in my civvies." He extended his free hand. "Can I help?"

Alan shook his head, regretting his use of four-letter words when he'd stumbled in the door. "Just the cup, thanks. I got this."

He hadn't known Chris and Rebecca were having company tonight. Eh, they probably didn't consider Father John company, more like family to Chris, a fact which, if Alan were honest, rankled him a bit. Alan and Chris had been close like that when they were kids. Up until the time Alan had started noticing girls.

His gaze darted toward the kitchen and then the hall. Where were Chris and Rebecca anyway?

As if he could read his mind, Father John said, "Chris is outside, grilling. And Rebecca . . ." His gaze shifted to the kitchen. "She's doing something with dinner. I offered to help, but . . ." He shrugged. "She knows I'm useless in the kitchen."

Alan pictured the charred frozen pizza he'd pulled from his oven a couple of weeks ago and couldn't stop the scoffing laugh that burst from his lips. "You think *you're* useless in the kitchen? You should see my wife in action." He bit his bottom lip, regretting the words. He loved Jamie, whatever her kitchen skills, or lack thereof.

Father John gave him a tight grin, probably unsure of how to react. Had Chris told him his marriage was on the rocks?

Awkward silence filled the small space between them as Alan yanked the plastic suitcase handle, making him acutely aware that the only thing he shared in common with Father John was the guy outside barbecuing their dinner.

He cast a furtive glance at the *padre*. Not a bad-looking guy. From the few times they'd been in Chris's company together, he knew only that he was smart and a huge baseball fan—specifically a Pittsburgh Pirates fan. He seemed at ease around people of all kinds, from the dirty-faced cherubs that tugged on his clerical robes to stooped, gray-haired old ladies in support hose and sensible shoes and even pimply teenagers who'd sooner have their parents glimpse their naked selfies than be caught in church.

No reason this guy couldn't have a girlfriend or wife. Probably a hot one at that. And yet, when he left tonight, he'd go to bed alone, just as he would for the rest of his life. Had he ever been with a woman, before his vows? Alan didn't know any guys in college who hadn't taken advantage of the plethora of willing females on campus, but then he hadn't known his own brother had remained a virgin until he'd married Rebecca mere months ago. As much as he loved and respected Chris, it still confounded him.

Just as he got the suitcase rolling, Rebecca emerged from the kitchen wiping her hands on the front of a peasant-style maternity blouse that gathered above her baby bump. "Alan. I thought I heard voices in here." She smiled, looking happier to see him than his own wife typically did. By the time he came home, Jamie was usually slouched on the couch, a glass of wine in one hand and the remote control in the other.

"How was work?"

No one had asked him that question in a long time, and he hadn't missed it. Talking about work made him irritable and edgy. He'd tried to put the huge sale he'd blown this morning out of his mind, but he couldn't shake the image of his customer's nasty snarl as he'd droned on about poor customer service, bait-and-switch, and making a report to the Better Business Bureau. "Same old thing. Customer ripped my head off, manager up my—" His gaze darted to Father John, and he clamped his mouth shut. "Sorry."

Father John grinned, grabbed an open bottle of beer—one of the popular ones from the brewery where Chris worked—from the end table and took a swig. "No apology necessary. I've had managers like that too." He gestured toward the kitchen and, Alan presumed, the small deck beyond. "I'll see how Chris is coming with the pork chops."

His hand grazed Rebecca's arm as he passed, and she flashed him a smile. Once the back door had shut, the small strap of bells attached to the top jingling to signal Father John's exit, Rebecca stepped closer.

She laid a hand over her abdomen, a gesture he'd seen her make more often of late, as if she were reminding herself of the baby beneath. "Your mom stopped by this afternoon to talk about Thanksgiving. You haven't told her, have you? About you and Jamie."

He raked a hand through his hair, letting it fall where it

lay. "No. You didn't say anything, did you?"

She shook her head, her shiny, brown locks swinging from side to side. "Not my place. But, Thanksgiving is next week. Your mom's expecting us. *All* of us. She wants you and Jamie to bring wine and those nuts you and Chris like. Have you talked to Jamie about it?"

"She doesn't respond to my texts." Of course, he couldn't remember when he'd last sent one. What could he say? He didn't even know what was wrong. "I'll try calling this weekend."

"I'd do it tonight if I were you. Your mom's having lunch with Jamie tomorrow."

8

An' Another Thing

Alan rested against the seat back and gazed at the familiar sights—the small patch of woods and homes he'd passed hundreds of times on bike rides and walks. The size of the homes struck him; they seemed much smaller than he remembered as a kid. Although he looked at them through grown-up eyes now, he still felt small—trapped and anxious, hoping this ruse succeeded.

Leaning forward between the front seats, Alan tapped Chris's arm. "Let me off here."

Rebecca shot him a quizzical look from the shotgun seat and then braced herself with a hand to the dashboard as Chris swerved to avoid a squirrel scampering across the street, forcing the car toward the curb. Piled leaves scattered like a flock of skittish birds.

Chris glanced in the rearview mirror and then braked. "Right here? We're an eighth of a mile from the house."

"Just stop, okay? Jamie's supposed to meet me here." Wait—was that her blue Honda Civic in the driveway? He squinted but couldn't make it out.

The car rolled along; Chris obviously having chosen to ignore Alan's instructions. Jamie's car came into clear view.

"Looks like she's already here." Rebecca shifted the apple pie on her lap and turned to face him. "Maybe you got your signals crossed?" The woman was so guileless, as if she couldn't imagine Jamie not doing as she'd said.

Not a chance he was mistaken. In the course of a short

and horribly stilted conversation, he'd made it plain to Jamie that he didn't want his parents to know they were living apart. She hadn't been happy about it, but she'd agreed to pretend everything was hunky-dory.

What gives, Jamie?

The aroma of roasted turkey wafted through the front door even before Alan pulled it open. He handed Chris and Rebecca his bottle of wine and jar of nuts and allowed them to enter ahead of him, hoping to keep his parents' attention focused on them while he located Jamie.

Mom, Dad, Chris, and Rebecca crowded around the kitchen island, hugging and making room for the apple pie amongst the casserole dishes and dessert plates on the counter. He glanced around, searching out Jamie. Naturally, she wouldn't be involved in the food preparation.

He found her in the living room, her back to him. A surge of wistful longing spread through his chest, only magnified by her presence in his childhood home amidst the cozy warmth of the holidays.

She stared at the photos on the fireplace mantle. A half-dozen framed photos sat alongside a dried flower arrangement and several small fall gourds. A decade-old family photo, his and Chris's high school graduation pictures, a shot of his parents at a friend's summer barbecue, and a set of wedding pictures. Jamie gazed at their wedding photo, a black-and-white photo taken immediately after the short civil ceremony.

Alan remembered only bits and snatches of his wedding day. The first half lingered in his memory as a happy blur. Jamie's red hair with golden streaks, sleek and pinned beneath a long veil. Her blue eyes shimmering as she repeated her vows. Hugs from aunts and people he'd never met before. Back claps from friends. The icky berry filling in the cake they'd paid way too much for. The way the left rental shoe made his instep ache with every step. The feel of the stiff fabric of Jamie's dress beneath his hand as they shared their first dance as husband and wife to the sounds of the Goo Goo Dolls.

He even remembered catching a glimpse of Chris and Rebecca on the edge of the dance floor engaged in a lip-lock. He'd never seen Chris like that with a girl—enthralled, looking like he held the winning ticket to the Powerball lottery and feared that at any misstep it might be taken away. Starry-eyed, he gazed at Rebecca—who, admittedly, looked beautiful, angelic even. Alan grinned, sure that he'd done his younger brother a big favor by pushing him to invite Rebecca even though they'd only gone on a few dates.

The wedding day details blurred after that, as if he were gazing through smeared aquarium glass into murky water. The edges—the particulars—were fuzzy, the feelings dulled.

The hotel contract for the ballroom went until midnight. After that, he and Jamie had headed to the bar. Megan's brother Tim had unfurled a wad of bills and proceeded to buy round after round, all the while inching closer to Alan's cousin Dylan's date, a petite, curvy blonde with the bluest eyes and whitest teeth he'd ever seen.

Sometime after two, he guessed, he and Jamie had stumbled up to the honeymoon suite. It had taken at least five minutes to get the keycard through the swiper, mainly because he lacked the coordination to line it up but also because Jamie leaned her full weight against him, throwing him even further off balance.

They'd collapsed on top of the king-size bed, ignoring the champagne and chocolate-covered strawberries laid out on the table. They'd dozed for a few minutes, he guessed, until Jamie snorted, waking him.

He rolled his head to the side, taking in her figure in that gorgeous dress that had nearly knocked him out when he'd spotted her at the end of the aisle. This was their wedding night. Drunk or not, one way or another, he was getting her out of that dress.

Despite her weak, mumbled protests, he fumbled with the loopy buttons running the length of her spine. His fingers felt more like the cumbersome paws of a costumed character. He was one of the Banana Splits trying to peel his bride out of her dress.

He murmured every hot thing he could think of in her ear. "C'mon, babe, it's our wedding night."

"Mmm . . ." Her half-smile slackened as the lure of sleep overtook her.

Frustrated, he lifted and straightened her shoulders to get a good look at her glassy eyes. "You wanna wait?" It was the last thing he wanted.

"No . . . it's our wedding night." But she toppled back on the bed, her arms flailing at her sides like the disjointed limbs of a discarded marionette.

Irritated and disappointed, he popped the champagne and chugged a glass. Maybe more subtle persuasion would put her in the mood. He crawled across the bed and planted a kiss on the back of her neck. He worked his way down along her shoulders, determined to rouse her enough to seal the deal, so to speak. Except it felt as if a heavy weight tugged his eyelids shut despite his buzzing head. Had he drunk so much they *couldn't* consummate their marriage on their wedding night? No way.

He wriggled out of his pants, and, stripped to his boxer shorts, scooted closer on the bed. Throwing his leg over hers, he wrapped himself around his bride and kissed her.

Finally, she moaned, and her obvious pleasure sparked his own interest. He groped her clumsily, his coordination still lacking. She moaned again, but this sounded of pain rather than pleasure. Jamie jerked out of his arms and scrambled for the bathroom.

The overpriced wedding cake with the icky berry filling made a second appearance. With the unpleasant memory near to overpowering the savory smells from the kitchen, Alan refocused on the present. On Jamie.

Her shoulders lifted then fell beneath her shimmery dark green blouse, as if she were sighing. Then she reached for the frame holding their picture and set it face down on the mantle.

A pang of sadness pricked him, intensified by her solemn appearance as she turned and faced him. Her straight red hair hung to her shoulders, tucked behind her ears on both sides. A few freckles stood out on her nose and cheeks, freckles he liked to trace with his thumb when she propped her head on his chest. He longed to go home, to hold her in bed at night, to feel whole again—loved and wanted.

"I had to come in." She must've heard him enter, because she didn't seem the least bit surprised to find him standing there. "Your dad was right behind me when I turned onto their street. Coming back from the grocery store with extra turkey broth."

He sunk his hands into his pockets. "What'd you tell them?"

She shrugged a shoulder. "That we rode separately. You were coming with Chris and Rebecca." Irritation shone in her sky-blue eyes. "I'm not going to lie, Alan."

He raised his hands in a defensive posture. "I didn't ask you to. I'd just rather not . . ." He glanced toward the kitchen. No one was paying attention, but he lowered his voice anyway. "They don't need to know all our business."

Her lips, coated in shiny pink gloss that he knew tasted like watermelon, twisted in a frown. "I'm not gonna spill details about our farce of a marriage, if that's what you're worried about, but the fact we're not living under the same roof is a pretty big deal."

Farce? Was it truly that bad? He hadn't thought so. They were experiencing a rough patch was all. Every marriage had those, right? "We can fix that. I'm ready to come home." She had no idea how ready. The mush factor at Chris and Rebecca's house bordered on nauseating.

He stepped closer and pulled his hands from his pockets. "Let's sit down and talk this through. You never even told me what it is—"

She huffed and brushed past him, headed toward the window overlooking the front yard.

He followed. "Seriously, Jamie. I need to hear what's wrong, and what we can do to fix it." He slid his hand across her back, the shimmery fabric of her blouse catching on the rough skin of his fingertips. "I love you. Talk to me."

She spun to face him. "Talk to you? All I've done is talk to you. Or maybe at you. You don't *listen*, Alan. You hear the words, you make the right response, but it never reaches here." She tapped her temple. "Or here." Her hand slid over her heart. "It's like you bide your time until I'm done flapping my gums, and then you just go on about whatever it is *you* want to say." Her hand waved aimlessly.

He massaged the tension from his neck. Was she right? Had he really not listened to her? His intention had never been to ignore her, but maybe he'd failed to recognize the importance of what she'd been telling him. When she'd told him time and again she wanted him to let her talk without trying to fix all of her problems, he'd taken her at her word. He let her talk, get it all out, and didn't bother so much with the details. Now she was angry he hadn't taken the details to heart.

"I'm sorry, Jamie. All the more reason for us—"

"Alan, Jamie, what can I get you to drink?" Dad sauntered in from the kitchen, ticking off the beverage options with his fingers. "A glass of wine, cider, ginger ale, Coke . . ."

Jamie's gaze flicked past Alan to his dad, her tone all sweetness. "I'd love some hot cider."

"Cider it is." Dad waited for Alan's answer.

"Uh, just a Coke. Thanks." He turned to Jamie, hoping to finish their conversation, but she'd already sashayed to the opposite end of the room where she hugged Rebecca and admired her growing baby bump.

The afternoon proceeded smoothly, and his parents gave no indication that they suspected any dissension between him and Jamie. Before dinner, they each took turns naming something they were thankful for this year. Chris and Rebecca, of course, said their marriage and the baby. Mom said everyone's good health, and Dad made some kind of cryptic remark about God's patience, which was weird because God wasn't a frequent guest at their table.

Jamie shot him a panicked glance then said she was grateful she still had her job after a companywide layoff.

Taking an uncalculated risk, Alan went with his heart. "I'm grateful for my wife." He turned in his seat so he could face Jamie, draping his arm over her seatback. The hairs on the back of his neck prickled with the awareness of his family members staring at him. Based on his past performances, they probably awaited the punch line. He had none. The only punch was the one to his gut when he thought of Jamie never welcoming him back to their home and their life together. "Whether I've had a crap day at work or made a giant sale, she's the one I want to come home to." He glanced up and caught Rebecca's tender expression before she batted her eyes and dipped her gaze.

Then he turned his focus solely to Jamie. "Always and forever."

Jamie's features softened, and he may have been mistaken, but it seemed as if her eyes grew watery too. She bit her lower lip.

He thought he'd say something more, for her ears only, about how much he missed her, but as a forkful of steaming stuffing reached his Mom's lips, Chris launched into a prayer and the moment passed.

Enough conversation, laughter, and delicious food filled the room that Alan almost believed life had returned to normal. Especially when after she'd served him a slice of Rebecca's apple pie with a scoop of vanilla ice cream, Jamie sat and slipped her hand into his beneath the table.

He and Jamie lingered over their desserts so long that everyone else had begun bussing the table, packing up leftovers, and arranging dishes in the dishwasher.

Jamie licked her fork clean, set it atop her plate, and pushed it forward. "Alan . . ."

He swallowed the hunk of crust in his mouth then reached for a glass of water, hoping to dislodge the lump in his throat. Looking at her expectantly, hope bloomed in his chest. "Yeah?"

"You're right. I—I think maybe I haven't communicated well with you. We *do* need to talk." She pinched a lock of hair between her thumb and finger and twisted it. "I want to tell you what's been bugging me all these months. I shouldn't . . . I shouldn't act like you can read my mind. Obviously, I need to be very plain."

He let a little grin slip. "I may not be as smart as I let on. Blunt is probably best with me."

She grinned back, and, for a second, everything in the world was right. "I know exactly how smart you are. You're right. Blunt is best." She jabbed him in the side with her elbow. "So, I've got something in the morning, but why don't you come home tomorrow afternoon, and we'll—"

"On my way to Virginia tomorrow, remember? The Dave Matthews Band concert?" By the look on her face, she'd forgotten. And his reminder was not welcome. "The tickets, they're in the fifth row, they're all paid for and—"

She pushed out of the chair so fast and with such force that the blond wheat back chair nearly toppled.

Alan steadied it as he jumped to his feet. "I'll be back Sunday and—"

Her hair swayed back and forth, her head shaking from side to side and her cheeks reddening to match her hair. "Just forget it." She bolted for the front closet and shoved coats out of the way until she found her black duffle coat. "If you'd rather hang out with thousands of dopeheads seeing the same concert for the hundredth time—"

He grabbed her arm, conscious that the conversation from the kitchen had petered out but not caring. "Will you *wait*? You can come with me and—"

"I am *not* coming with you. Let's just forget about it. You know what you can do to *fix this*, as you said?" Anger flushed her cheeks as she shoved her arms into her jacket.

Alan stood by, helpless, wanting to lift the sleeve over her shoulder but not wanting her to leave. "Don't do this, Jamie. Please."

A sheen of moisture glazed her blue eyes, and a tear escaped. She brushed it away with a rough jab of her hand. "Grow up, Alan. It's that simple. Grow. Up." She turned the corner and shouted her thanks and goodbyes, then tore out of the house, the door slamming behind her.

A blast of cold air emphasized the heat in Alan's cheeks and ears. He let his head loll backward and groaned, deflated. Not only had the gulf between him and Jamie widened, but it had all gone down in front of his family. He ran a hand through his hair and dragged himself to the kitchen, where his parents stood alongside the kitchen island snapping shut Tupperware lids. Chris picked through a bowl of after-dinner mints, and Rebecca transferred the remaining slice of her pie to a smaller plate.

"Sorry." It was the only thing he knew to say. He'd likely ruined everyone's Thanksgiving, bringing the light conversation and easy family camaraderie to a grinding halt.

Dad stacked one container on top of another, wiped his hands on a striped yellow dishcloth and whispered something in Mom's ear. She nodded, and then Dad came at him, that Ward Cleaver, paternal look in his eye. "I'll take out the garbage. Alan, would you grab the recyclables bin?"

"Yes, sir." And just like that, Alan was twelve years old again, caught playing his Game Boy under the covers. His stomach knotted, anticipating the lecture he knew awaited him outside.

9
True Reflections

Megan depressed the pedal on the garbage can and scraped the remnants of her restaurant takeout Thanksgiving dinner into the trash. Dry turkey and congealed cranberries dropped like chunks of lead atop crumpled napkins. *Yuck.*

Before the miasma of cast-off food could make her stomach turn, she shifted her gaze to the dining room. Tim, her mom, and her mom's sister, Trudy, sat sipping coffee and awaiting a slice of the pumpkin pie Megan had picked up at the grocery store. Tim said something she couldn't quite hear, and Mom and Aunt Trudy laughed. Everyone was so darn . . . *happy.* Why did that disgust her?

Tim had always been a glass-half-full kind of guy, but he'd been downright chipper all day. More troublesome than his obnoxious joyful veneer was the change in his . . . well, *him.* His edge had been dulled. A glimmer of compassion tempered his sarcasm. His presence held a gravity she hadn't recognized before. He'd *hugged* her when she'd come to the door. Not a bear hug that squeezed her ribs until she begged for mercy. Not a back-slapping hug meant to knock the wind out of her. Not even a meaningless side hug meant to suffice as an obligatory holiday greeting. A real hug—intentional, affectionate, warm, and protective—topped with a kiss to her temple.

Had he undergone rehab or a lobotomy?

The hug had just been a prelude to the real kicker, which

came before dinner.

Tim had cleared his throat and tapped the stem of his glass with the end of his spoon.

Megan stopped, mid-sip, and turned her attention to him, clueless as to what important announcement he had to make. Maybe he wanted to thank them for their support while he was in rehab. Or maybe he had news about his recent job interview.

He extended a hand to her and to Aunt Trudy, on his opposite side. He breathed deeply, almost as if he were nervous, and squeezed Megan's fingers. A quick glance at his jittery knee and forced smile confirmed her suspicion. What would make him so anxious?

"If you don't mind, I'd like to, uh, do something different this year. I-I'd like to lead us in prayer."

Megan felt her eyes grow wide as saucers. It's not as if she were an atheist or anything, she mostly just didn't care. She didn't *do* religion. Her family didn't *do* religion. At least they hadn't. Before now.

Aunt Trudy's expression betrayed nothing, and Mom appeared unflustered, as if they prayed before meals all the time. "Go ahead, Tim," she said.

The prayer consisted of what to Megan's mind were Evangelical buzz words: praise, glory, worship, blah, blah, blah. Mercifully, it was quick. Now she only feared that once the pie was consumed, Tim would be emboldened to proceed with an altar call.

She removed the pumpkin pie from its box, sliced it into even pieces, then grabbed a tub of whipped topping from the refrigerator and carried it to the table. The first slice fell apart as she lifted it onto the plate, but knowing Tim wouldn't care, she piled it high with a giant-sized dollop of whipped topping.

"Thanks. Looks good. Where'd you get it?" Tim

examined the pie, dipping his fork into the topping and mashing the pumpkin filling.

"Rieser's Market." The old, family-owned grocery store was out of her way, but it *did* have the best bakery and butcher shop around. Plus, she knew the store and its layout better than any other, giving her the ability to get in and out in a flash. She'd visited all hours of the day and night for as long as Chris had been employed there, which had been longer than she'd expected.

She met Tim's gaze as she handed pie to her mom and aunt. His knowing look held more pity than smugness. She preferred the smugness to what she imagined was running through his mind. *Poor Megan, still pining over a man—a married man—who never gave her a second look. Haunting all the places he frequented.* She averted her gaze and slid a plate in front of her own seat.

Megan tuned out of the conversation, which from the few words she'd heard, seemed to revolve around the fifty-some acres of farmland down the road that were destined to become another strip mall. Didn't they have plenty already? Tomorrow would be a mess, Black Friday shoppers everywhere. Hopefully by the time she met Jamie for coffee, it wouldn't be so crazy.

Guilt niggled her conscience. Jamie . . . had she and Alan spoken? Did she know he'd accompanied her home? Or that Megan had messed with him a little by trying to pull him onto the bed with her?

"Megan. Are you listening?" Tim's voice reached her a millisecond before the bit of pumpkin filling flung from his fork.

"Hey! Watch it." She snatched a paper napkin from the center of the table and dabbed at the little glob of pumpkin staining her placemat.

His devilish grin almost made her smile. *Almost.* "Had to

get your attention somehow." His grin faded as he fidgeted with his glass, twirling it aimlessly. "This is important."

What now? The afternoon had consisted of successive disappointments beginning with the lack of wine, in deference to Tim, followed by the bland meal, and she feared it would culminate in whatever Tim was about to share.

"First, I want to thank you all for your support . . . with the rehab. Maybe you don't think it was necessary . . ." His gaze homed in on Megan. "I needed it. I'm a better man. Or at least I'm trying to be." He let out a breath and rested his hands in his lap, a smile spreading across his face, lighting his eyes.

Megan fidgeted under his gaze. As far as she was concerned, the rehab was a waste of time, and this girl he'd mentioned, she seemed to be the impetus for it. Trying to make him into something he wasn't. He didn't need fixing—

"There're more changes coming, and I hope you'll support those too." Again, his piercing gaze landed on Megan.

She bristled, sensing she wouldn't like what he was going to say.

"I'm moving. Not far or anything, just Lancaster." He rested his folded arms on the table.

Lancaster? What—he was turning Amish now? He couldn't even grow a decent beard, as evidenced by the scruff on his face more than three weeks into No-Shave November.

"Moving?" Mom's eyes widened, and she reached for Tim's hand and squeezed his fingers. "Why?"

He shrugged. "A fresh start? I need a new environment. I don't want to fall into old patterns and habits. Besides . . ." He squared his shoulders and gave them a confident smile.

His eyes held a peaceful look that Megan hadn't seen there before. "It's time for a change."

Mom sipped her coffee and nodded.

Aunt Trudy bobbed her head too. "I think that's a smart idea." She scraped the remains of her pie onto her fork. "And it's not far at all."

They could play nice about it all they wanted. Megan wasn't buying it. A suspicion creep-crawled up her spine, and her eyes narrowed.

"It's *her*, isn't it? This girl. The one that dragged you off to rehab as if you were a drunk. The one that's filled your head with all this religious hooey." Megan shoved away her remaining pie, her appetite gone.

"Megan . . ." Mom's tone said she didn't want an argument.

Tough. Someone had to give Tim the truth, and it might as well be Megan. "No, Mom. Are you hearing this? She's forcing him—"

"No one forces me to do anything." Tim's strident voice matched her own. "Yes, Holly factored into my decision, but it's my own. And I *was* a drunk. Not a falling down, sloppy drunk, but, yeah, drunk. A lot." His gaze shifted to Mom and Aunt Trudy. "I didn't want to get into all this." He sighed, his shoulders sagging. "I'm moving a half-hour away. It's not like I'm shipping off to Zimbabwe or something."

"Of course not," Mom said, clearing her throat and shooting a pointed glance at Megan. *Keep the peace* could've been Mom's personal motto. "I didn't know you and Holly were serious."

"We're not. Not yet anyway, but I like her. A lot. And if she's spurred any changes in me, they're good ones." He shot a glare toward Megan. "I've never met anyone like her. She's got this thing about her, this joy." He shook his head, as if in disbelief. "She's content. I like being around her. I like *myself* when I'm around her."

Megan huffed and folded her arms across her chest. *Puh-leez.*

Aunt Trudy chuckled. "Oh, that's how it begins." She turned the band on her ring finger, the one she continued to wear though Uncle Rich had been gone more than two years now.

Tim ducked his head, his neck reddening. "Yeah, maybe." He glanced up at Megan. "Anyway, I wanted you to know. And I want you to meet Holly too." His gaze flicked to Mom's. "Maybe Sunday? She's visiting family in New Jersey now, but she'll be back Saturday."

"That sounds wonderful, Tim. I'll be here." Mom's chest swelled with what? Pride?

Megan shoved away from the table, scooping up dirty dishes and flatware. She spun toward the kitchen, a dirty napkin flying to the floor. The dishes landed in the sink with a clatter, and her vision blurred. Tears? What was wrong with her?

She brushed her eyes with the back of her hand, conscious of Tim's soft footfalls behind her. He grabbed her arm and turned her to face him, her shoulder tensing at his touch.

His features were pinched, irritation in the slant of his brows. "I expected more of you, Megan. Why can't you be happy for me? I'm getting my life together. I met someone I care about. Are you jealous? Bitter? Or are you just a—"

She swatted his arm. "Don't you dare. I'm just . . . I don't know, okay? I don't like all these changes. I liked the way things were." He could take his cues from the self-help section of the bookstore if he wanted, but she resented his accusations and his insinuation that she needed to change too.

Tim glanced at the floor between them then back at her. "Maybe you oughta think about that, huh? Why do you want me trapped, unhappy, in a downward spiral? Why, Megan? What does it say about you and how you're living?" His features hard and unforgiving, he returned to the living room where she overheard him make his goodbyes.

Megan flicked the faucet on and ran her hand through the stream of water, waiting for it to warm. Good riddance. Maybe now she could have a glass of wine.

10

Let You Down

The large blue container of glass and plastic rattled as Alan hoisted it through the back door, leaving behind the sounds of laughter and clanging pots and pans. He followed Dad, who tugged a heavy-duty drawstring garbage bag at his side. In one deft movement, Dad swung the bag up and into the open trash can, the odor of onion and turkey scraps filling the air. Alan upended his container, and glass wine bottles, an empty plastic pretzel barrel, and a slew of water bottles slid out, followed by a couple of newspapers and a pile of junk mail.

While his dad closed the containers, Alan gazed over the backyard. The grass had turned sallow and the nearly bare trees allowed a peek through the woods at the trails he and Chris had traversed countless times as kids. Life had been so simple then; his biggest troubles had been pre-algebra and Chris encroaching on his space, both of which were eased by tromping through golden leaves covering loamy paths.

"My only question is: why didn't you go after her?" Dad's deep voice was firm but more curious than accusatory. He rolled the trash and recyclable receptacles into place, the plastic wheels crunching over fall leaves and stray stones, and leaned against the vinyl fence post that helped hide the cans from view.

His chest aching with a mixture of shame, embarrassment, and lingering anger at how Jamie had stormed out, Alan boosted himself onto the deck box where his parents stored charcoal and grill tools. "I guess I didn't see the point. Not to mention, I don't have my car."

Dad's brow furrowed. "You're living apart, aren't you?"

Alan nodded, his gaze slipping to his loafers.

"Who left?"

"Me. Not that I wanted to. She pretty much tossed me out the door with a duffel bag of stuff and the clothes on my back." He shivered more from the memory of standing on his stoop barechested in the cold than the cool breeze now lifting his hair.

"I wish you'd asked your mom and me to stay here." Contrary to his words, the set of his jaw and his pinched brow didn't exactly scream "welcome."

He hadn't thought his parents might be hurt by his decision to keep things quiet and stay with Chris. He'd taken the path of anticipated least resistance, knowing Chris—

"We would've turned you right around and sent you home, where you belong. How are you supposed to work things out if you're not communicating? I imagine there're some situations where a separation is necessary, but—"

"What would you have me do?" Alan shoved off the box and stood an arm's length away and a few inches taller than his dad, but felt a full foot smaller despite his irritation. "Force my way back in?"

Dad's head moved back and forth, ever so slowly. "And, let me guess. You're boarding with your brother. He and his brand-new wife, married less than six months, pregnant, still adjusting to each other's routines and habits."

Dad didn't need to worry about that. The "adjustment" seemed to be going swimmingly. He hadn't heard a raised voice from either of them the entire time he'd been there. They nearly cooed at one another with their sweet nothings. Not to mention all the physical contact. He'd never taken either one of them for the touchy-feeling type, but they were stuck together like Velcro most of the time. The kisses, embraces, backrubs, day in and day out. Alan felt like a starving man seated at a six-course banquet where his tablemates gorged and feasted.

"I try to steer clear of them."

Dad cocked an eyebrow. "You're eating, sleeping, and showering there. Their house is small, maybe half the size of this place." He gestured toward the spacious two-story home Alan had taken for granted. "Doesn't do much for privacy."

Alan huffed. His marriage was falling apart, and Dad only seemed to care whether he was disturbing Chris and Rebecca. He turned and strode back toward the house. "Fine," he snapped. "I'll go find a park bench so I don't bother the lovebirds."

"Alan." The authority in Dad's voice stopped him in his tracks. "I don't want to interfere. Whatever's between you and Jamie is your business, not mine. Not your mother's. Not your brother's."

Alan turned slowly, some of the tension in his neck and shoulders easing.

Dad ambled toward him. "If it's okay, I just want to remind you of a couple things."

Alan nodded. He bristled at being lectured but knew that's not what Dad intended. Truth was, he'd lap up any advice his father offered. They'd butted heads from time to time, especially when Alan had been a teenager, but he admired his dad in a dozen different ways, especially as a paragon of the faithful, loving husband.

"First, those vows you made were forever." Dad slung an arm around his shoulder, buoying Alan's sagging spirit. "Second, marriage has its ups and downs. Lots of them.

That's to be expected. They're opportunities to grow together, not drift apart." He smiled, gazing out over the yard. "Take it from someone who's done his share of drifting. And growing."

Seconds past. He'd finished doling out wisdom already? "Is that it?"

"Yep." He squeezed Alan's shoulder then let his arm fall to his side and slid his hand into the pocket of his khaki pants. "How's work?"

So much for being buoyed. Work might be the sandbag that finally pulled him under. "My sales have gone from sixth in the region last quarter to third from the bottom so far this quarter."

"What happened?" Dad stopped outside the door, glancing through the window.

Inside, Mom was all smiles, and Chris had his face pressed to Rebecca's baby bump, probably babbling at the baby as he often did these days. Could the kid even hear him yet?

Alan studied the concrete slab beneath them, kicking away an acorn with his shoe. At least Dad, having made a career of sales, would understand. Chris never got it. He went to work and whether he had a lousy week or dealt with a boatload of nut jobs, he still got paid. Jamie listened to his work woes and tried to sympathize, but her pat answer was "find a different job." As if his email box were clogged with messages from recruiters offering high-income, low-stress, no-travel positions. But Dad, he got it.

"They changed the commissions. I've got to have 25 percent more new customers than before. My manager took half of my leads and gave them to a newbie. And they outsourced our customer service to India, and everyone's complaining about the wait time and support. I'm losing income faster than I'm losing hair." He met Dad's eyes, and the reason he didn't want to admit tumbled out. "And maybe I'm distracted and unmotivated."

Dad twisted the doorknob and held the door open for him. "Well, you've been doing this long enough to know how it goes. Is your resumé up to date?"

Alan sighed. "I should include the sales training we did last year." He was about to cross the threshold when his phone vibrated in his pocket, and he glanced at the screen. His heart tripped. A text message from Jamie. Anxious to read the message, Alan moved away from the door and glanced at Dad. "I'll be right in." He held up the phone. "Message from Jamie."

"Time to make amends," Dad said with a tight smile before he shuffled inside, the door clicking behind him.

Alan scanned the message, hope blossoming in his chest.

Sorry that happened in front of the fam. Should've done that in private.

He let out the breath he'd been holding. His thumbs hovered over the phone as he formulated his response. Dad was right. They needed to get under the same roof. He'd get Chris to run him home and figure out how to get his car and stuff later. He started tapping: *Sorry too. Let's talk. I can come now—*

Before he could finish and hit send, another message came.

Talked with my mom. Knee replacements are moved up. One bathroom on second floor at her place. She's gonna come here for recovery. I'll take family leave. With you gone, works out perfect.

His thumbs froze. Perfect? For her mom maybe. Not for him. But what could he say? He and his mother-in-law weren't on the best terms to begin with. She'd always wanted *more* for Jamie. Someone with more income, more sophistication, "more attentive."

If he refused to allow her to stay there, he risked making Jamie angrier. If he insisted on moving back, what would be the point? Jamie would be busy serving as caregiver, and they'd still not be alone together. Neither scenario boded well for reconciliation.

Still, he had to try, didn't he? Show her how important she was to him and how much their marriage meant. He typed quickly, hoping to forestall any more messages on her end.

I'll help any way I can. Let's talk. I can come now.

He waited for her response, pacing toward the deck box and back. He glanced at the time. Dinner was done, and Rebecca was probably tired; she sometimes conked out on the couch this time of day. He'd just get Chris to run him by—

Jamie's response came. *Don't bother. I'm beat, and you need your rest for travel tomorrow.*

He gritted his teeth. Alan couldn't be certain since it was a text message, but he guessed the last remark dripped so heavily with sarcasm it left a puddle behind.

The door squeaked open, and Chris poked his head out. "Hey, Mom's got these Minute-to-Win-It games she wants us to do." He rolled his eyes, but his grin gave away that he didn't really mind. Life still looked swell through his rose-colored glasses. "You comin' in?"

"I'll be right there." Why not top off the night with yet more humiliation as he tried to thread beads onto a dry spaghetti noodle using only his teeth or unwrap Hershey kisses while wearing oven mitts?

He stared at the phone, his thumbs tapping out a message. Fine, he'd stay away. For now. But, he wouldn't give up that easily. *I'll call Sunday. I love you.*

He waited several minutes for Jamie's reply. None came, so he pasted on a fake smile and headed back inside, rubbing his hands together. "You guys ready? Ready for me to crush you?"

11

I'll Back You Up

Patrons shook out their umbrellas and stamped their feet as they entered the coffee shop, their plastic shopping bags glistening with droplets of water. Thunder rumbled in the distance, and Megan, seated at a table for two, glanced at the sky. A dark mass of gray-black clouds threatened to unleash another torrent of blowing rain.

A quiver of anxiety passed through her. She didn't know what to expect from the afternoon. Jamie had been distant for weeks, obviously not sharing the extent of her marital troubles. And then to have Alan fill her in, while Megan had been looped, only added to the awkwardness.

C'mon, Jamie. She glanced at her phone, checking for a message. Nothing.

Less than five minutes later, Jamie squeezed through the front door, seeking shelter from the deluge. She slipped off the hood of her rain jacket and glanced around the café.

Megan waved, trying to get her attention. Using her foot, she pushed out the metal chair across the small, round table.

Jamie's gaze snapped to Megan's waving hand, and she made a beeline for her. "Hey, sorry I'm late." Her gaze flicked to the large plate glass windows being pelted by sheets of driving rain. "Traffic's nuts out there." She slid her sopping rain jacket over the seat back and sat, pushing strands of damp hair from her face.

"No problem." Megan toyed with her bracelets while Jamie situated herself and then turned her attention back to the table.

Jamie's face seemed thinner; her eyes wearier than she'd ever seen them. Easy going and rock steady, she had seemed immune to the emotional ups and downs Megan weathered. Jamie had always been self-assured and optimistic. She loved Alan fiercely, and that was the only aspect of her life in which she'd ever seemed vulnerable.

Jamie eyed the line for coffee then grabbed a stray napkin from the table and wiped the rainwater from her face. "Thanks for meeting me. Did you have a good Thanksgiving?"

Megan shrugged. "Tim sobered up, found God, and decided to move away from everyone he knows and loves." No use beating around the bush.

Jamie's eyes widened. "Wow. I guess that's all good, right? How far is he moving?"

"Just to Lancaster. No biggie." She examined her peeling nail polish, making a mental note to apply a fresh coat later. Not wanting to think about Tim, let alone talk about him, she turned the conversation back on Jamie. "How was your Turkey Day?"

Her mournful sigh said it all. "Awkward. Then . . . kinda hopeful. And then not so good." She winced. "I stormed out of the house, in front of Alan's parents and everything."

"Ouch. What happened?"

"I don't know if Alan told you, whenever it was you saw him, but, I . . ." Her gaze dropped, and if the slump of her shoulders was any indication, her confidence faltered. "We're not living together."

"He told me. But not much else." A twinge of guilt stung Megan as she recalled Alan lifting her feet onto the bed and her trying to pull him down, but she worked to keep her expression neutral.

"I miss him so much, Megan. I do. And being with him . .

." She fidgeted with the cuffs of her cable-knit sweater. "It felt good. I thought we could talk and then . . . he's still going to a concert this weekend."

"Let me guess. Dave Matthews Band?" She knew all about Alan's dedication to hitting as many of their concerts as he could.

"Bingo. Priorities, y'know?" Jamie's gaze flicked to the line at the counter. "I'll get us something. Coffee? Latte? Espresso?"

"Surprise me." Megan glanced at her phone, looking without really seeing. She scrolled through her Twitter feed. "God Saves" was trending right behind "Black Friday." And sure enough, Tim had contributed to the trend. She laid the phone face down and nudged it forward on the table.

In a few minutes, Jamie returned and handed her a steaming drink. She sat, her back rigid as she sipped her coffee.

"So, you said you could use a friend. Do you want to talk about things?" Megan warmed her hands on the cup and stared at Jamie, curious as to what she wanted to share with her.

Jamie pushed her cup forward and rested her elbows on the table. "Yeah. I'm sorry I kinda fell off the face of the earth. It's just tough talking about it."

Megan nodded and waited for her to continue.

"Not because it's so emotional. It's tough because I don't know who to talk to." She leaned back in the seat and sighed. "Our friends are all mutual friends. I don't want to sound like I'm bad-mouthing Alan when you're his friend. And your brother's his friend. Rebecca's a good listener, but she's married to his brother."

Thanks for the reminder. Megan kept her eyes wide and sympathetic despite the stab of jealousy Rebecca's name always caused.

"But I have to talk to *someone*, y'know?" Jamie's brows lifted in a hopeful expression as if confirmation and the opportunity to unburden her heart were key to the solace she sought.

And Megan held that key in her hand. Not that she wanted it. She deplored being caught between Alan and Jamie, but Jamie obviously needed a listening ear.

"If you need to blow off steam, I won't hold it against Alan. Unless he deserves it, in which case I'll be happy to hold his size elevens to the fire." She didn't add that she'd relish every second of it after the hard time he'd given her at the bar.

"Thanks." Jamie sipped her coffee slowly then pursed her lips and stared at the cup, as if she were gathering her thoughts. "Bottom line is I'm afraid he's gonna flake out on me or leave. Just . . ." She made diminishing circles with her hand. ". . . drift off and find someone new."

Megan scrunched her brow. "Has he cheated?" Granted, she didn't know Alan *that* well, but given his reaction to her teasing, she figured his marriage meant something to him.

Jamie shook her head. "No. Never."

"Then why would you think . . .?" She let the question hang as she tried to understand why Jamie would worry about what seemed like a non-issue.

"It's the baby thing."

"Baby thing?" As she spoke, a baby cried from the opposite end of the shop, drowning out the nasally crooning of an aging rock star coming from the overhead speakers. "Are you pregnant?"

"No. But Alan's ready to try." Jamie turned her paperboard cup in circles. "It's not that I don't want a baby. I do. And he *says* he does, but I don't know. Does he want to be a dad or is it like moving in or getting married? Just the next thing we're *supposed* to do? We find out Chris's going to be a dad and suddenly Alan wants to impregnate me, like, yesterday."

"You think he wants to have a baby because of sibling rivalry?" That seemed a stretch. Competition about grades, sports, or girls, yeah. Income and status? Okay. A baby? Being that Megan had never given thought to a baby beyond tossing the negative pregnancy test into the trash can, she'd never considered it.

"When you say it like that, I'm not sure. But even if it's not that, c'mon, what are Alan's priorities?" She ticked them off on her fingers. "Following the Dave Matthews Band, having a good time, and keeping things light. Not exactly top qualifications for paternal stability."

Megan saw her point—to a point. Yeah, Alan was easy-going and liked to party. Sure, he went to a lot of concerts. But he also held down a job, made decent money, and had committed himself to Jamie, however flimsy his original intentions had been. His dad was a great father by all accounts. She sensed Jamie's fears, while not unfounded, may be misplaced or, at the least, exaggerated. What really made her fearful of motherhood?

"Dumb question, but have you talked to him about it?" Calling it dumb would soften the blow, Megan hoped. Sometimes the obvious had to be asked.

Jamie's shifting glance and fidgeting hands said she'd booted her confused, baby-badgering husband out the door without an honest admission of her reluctance. "Of course," she said, her tone curt but her eyes never meeting Megan's.

"Jamie." She waited until her friend's eyes lifted. "I hope you guys work it out. I know he's not perfect. And you're not perfect—" She held a hand up as Jamie opened her mouth to object, her lips curled in a smile. "Though pretty darn close." Megan grinned. "But, you're pretty perfect together. And I know he loves you."

Jamie's eyes misted and she pursed her lips. "I love him too, overgrown kid or not."

Megan ignored her jab at Alan, reached across the table, and squeezed Jamie's hand as her phone chimed, signaling a text message. She retracted her hand and glanced at the message.

Alan? She didn't even realize he had her number. What could he possibly want?

She glanced at Jamie, who'd blinked back her tears and was zippering something into her purse. What would she think if she knew her husband was texting her friend, right across the table?

"Listen, I've gotta go." Jamie grabbed her nearly-dry raincoat from the back of her chair and slid her arms into it. "I want to touch base with my mom. She had an appointment with her orthopedist this morning. She's gotta schedule a double knee replacement and then she's recovering at my place. Y'know, while Alan's . . . gone."

Megan nodded. How had Alan taken *that* news, that his mother-in-law would be moving into his house while he'd been evicted? Or had Jamie even told him?

If Megan was going to fret about anyone's happiness, it should be her own. She hadn't found the magic prescription so far. Men and martinis offered only a short-term fix. Marriage was a crap shoot. Her parents' marriage was a disaster. Aunt Trudy and Uncle Rich's had been a fairy tale. Alan and Jamie, practically newlyweds, couldn't keep it together. Chris and Rebecca seemed ridiculously happy, but what marriage with Chris Reynolds as half the equation wouldn't be? Tim seemed happy, after his come-to-Jesus moment. Who knew if that would last?

She stuffed her used napkin into her cup as Jamie tugged her hood over her head and exited the store into the rain. The storm outside had eased and the blowing ceased. Had their conversation helped ease Jamie's personal turmoil? Doubtful.

How had Megan got thrust into the middle of it all, with Alan becoming her drinking buddy and Jamie the other member of her coffee klatch? The less she got involved in their marital drama the better, but she got the sinking feeling she was already in deeper than her thigh-high stockings.

12

Snow Outside

February

Snowflakes fell in thick clumps on the lawn, blanketing the icy crust of last week's snowfall with a fresh coating of white fluff. Alan's breath fogged the living room window of Chris and Rebecca's house, but the cold pane felt good against his achy head.

A snowblower engine hummed from down the block, and a boy bundled head to toe in winter garb chased a black and white puppy, kicking up clouds of snow.

Under the weight of his troubles, Alan turned away from the peaceful scene and leaned against the sill. A bouquet of red roses, still thriving two weeks after Valentine's Day, sat on the end table. In the corner beside them, a long, rectangular box leaned against the wall. The UPS guy had delivered some kind of playpen thing yesterday, expecting a signature while Alan stumbled through a phone interview with a recruiter.

Three months had passed since his manager had informed him he'd been terminated after not meeting his sales goal two quarters in a row. He'd sent a panicked text to Megan on Black Friday, hoping she had a lead on a sales position. Hers was a support position, but the public relations/advocacy firm she worked for had a few sales-type account management positions.

It had been worth a shot, he'd thought. But after a month of contacting just about everyone he knew and scouring online job listings day in and day out, he'd taken a retail position at a big-box electronics store. It wounded his pride and ate into his job search time, but at least he could offer Chris and Rebecca something for letting him crash at their place. After all, Chris had not-so-subtly tossed around the word "rent" more than once while poring over his and Rebecca's finances.

A light flicked on in the kitchen, and the gurgle and hiss of the coffee machine working told him Chris was up. Rebecca had stopped drinking coffee months ago, saying the taste didn't appeal to her anymore.

Gripping a mug with one hand and scratching his belly absently with the other, Chris rounded the corner, his gaze fixed on the snowfall. "How many inches did we get overnight?"

Alan glanced out the window from where he stood alongside it. "Four more, maybe?"

Chris nodded and blew on his coffee, steam wafting from his mug. "Think maybe you can manage to shovel the walk this time or should I tell Rebecca to drag her thirty-six-week-pregnant body out here and get a move on it?"

Back to that, were they? Alan gritted his teeth. "How long are you gonna beat that dead horse, huh?" Last week, Chris had come home to Rebecca shoveling the front steps while he sat in front of the blaring TV in sleep pants and an undershirt, feet up, popping potato chips into his mouth. It hadn't been a pretty picture, and Alan regretted it.

Heck, he hadn't even known she'd gone out there. Rebecca had mentioned something about clearing the front before Chris got home, and he'd said he'd get to it, but he'd been engrossed in season three of *Parks and Recreation*, and it had slipped his mind.

Despite her condition, she insisted on doing things herself, so he guessed she got tired of waiting and went out the back, shoveling her way around to the front, unbeknownst to Alan. Yeah, he should've done it right off when she first mentioned it, but, darn it, he'd been out all day knocking on doors, resume in hand. Chris acted like Alan had harnessed Rebecca, lashed her with a whip, and forced her to dig out from under a foot of heavy snow.

Chris normally exhibited more patience than anyone he knew, but lately, whether it was the impending birth, Alan's presence, or something else, it seemed his fuse had been clipped so short a mere static charge resulted in a massive explosion.

Rebecca remained as pleasant and accommodating as ever, but even she couldn't cool the roiling boil bubbling between the brothers. If they were going to go another round now, he hoped she'd sleep through it. She tended to sleep later these days.

"Dead horse, huh? Oh, I'm gonna flog it a good, long time. Until you make up for it and then some." Chris took a long drink, set the mug on the coffee table and flopped onto the couch. He grabbed the instructions for assembling the playpen thing from the table and flipped through them, turning it over and upside down before concentrating on the diagrams and tiny text.

"Fine. I'll get dressed and shovel now." He pushed off the wall, pacing in front of the window. "Then I'll go and, I don't know, stand in the street with a signboard saying, 'Need work.' In a residential neighborhood . . . on a Saturday . . . in the snow."

Chris didn't look up. "Yeah, while you're at it, why don't you find somewhere else to crash?"

Alan nodded in an exaggerated fashion and propped his hands on his hips. So *that* was it. He'd worn out his welcome. "Yeah, 'cause I've got so much cash rolling in."

For someone who'd woken up minutes ago, the fire in Chris's eyes gleamed with intensity. "Then why don't you, oh, I don't know . . ." He flung his hand in the air. "GO

HOME?" He flipped a page in the instruction manual, which he held in front of his face.

Alan stilled for a full three seconds, his jaw clenched, his teeth grinding. Go home? He'd never wanted to leave in the first place. He reached forward and whacked the bottom of the directions, causing them to smack Chris's forehead.

Chris tossed the booklet onto the couch and leapt to his feet, lunging for Alan and wrenching his arms as he tried to escape.

Shooting a hard glare, Alan tried twisting his arms free. Were they really gonna do this? Could he take Chris? They hadn't gotten into a scuffle since Chris's college years. Chris had been a little on the scrawny side back then, but he'd added some muscle.

Alan swiveled around, finally yanking his arm from Chris's grasp. "You want me to leave? I'll go."

Chris ground his jaw, probably determining how far he wanted to take this. He crossed his arms over his chest, his biceps bulging beneath the sleeves of his white undershirt. Yeah, he'd gained some muscle. "No, you know what I want? I want you to think about someone besides yourself for a change. Maybe pick up some of the slack that I'm sick and tired of carrying." His voice elevated.

The bed creaked down the hall, and Alan's gaze darted in that direction. He shot Chris a narrowed look, but it went unnoticed. He purposefully kept his voice low, though it strained with irritation. "What are you talking about?"

Chris scoffed. "What am I talking about?" He shook his head. "When Dad had his leg in that immobilizer thing in September, who cut his grass? Who cleaned out their gutters?" He stepped closer, encroaching on Alan's personal space. "All while, you know what my wife was doing?"

Let's see. Probably preparing a home-cooked meal, baking a gourmet dessert, and scattering rose petals all over your bed? At least that's what he *wanted* to say, but he clamped his lips shut.

When he got no response, Chris resumed his rant. "Rebecca spent the day alternately hanging over the toilet with morning sickness and blowing her nose 'cause she caught some cold. You don't think I wanted to be here to take care of her? I was pretty cheesed off about the whole thing. You know why? You remember what you were doing that weekend?"

Alan didn't give an inch. Not in space and not in his unflinching stare. He'd beat Chris at staring contests since before they'd given up training wheels. For the life of him, he couldn't remember that weekend. How would he have known what Chris had been doing?

Answering his own question, Chris waved an arm in the air, his voice louder still. "You're off at some Dave Matthews concert with Tim and whoever else, hanging out at bars, goin' wherever, and after I'm done at Mom and Dad's, I come home to a sick wife, filthy dishes in the sink, and a pile of dirty laundry. Then guess who calls me. *Your* wife."

Ah, that weekend. Alan still couldn't recall details, but he remembered what he'd come home to, too: Jamie, peeved that he'd been hundreds of miles away when the washing machine had flooded the laundry room. His gaze fell to his feet, and he raked a hand through his hair, pushing a lock from his line of vision.

"She didn't know where to find the shut off valve when the washer busted." He poked Alan's chest, then shoved, two-handed.

Alan stumbled back, heat creeping up his neck. "You're gonna be sorry you did that." Maybe Chris had a point, and maybe he had good reason. Maybe the fact that Rebecca had become a ticking hormonal time bomb frayed Chris's nerves.

Alan couldn't have cared less. His stressors exceeded Chris's, hands down. Chris had a job to go to and a wife to come home to. At present, Alan lacked both. If anyone needed to blow off steam, it was Alan. His blood pressure must be sky high with the level of near-constant frustration he endured. Not to mention the sexual frustration. He hadn't gone this long without sex since he was a pimply teenager dependent on cheap alcohol and a smokin' playlist to facilitate his satisfaction. It didn't help that he slept mere feet away, separated by only a thin wall, from the happy honeymooners, more often than not with his head buried in a pillow so he wouldn't overhear their conversation—or anything else.

He pushed Chris backward onto the couch, tackling him as they went down, their legs banging against the coffee table.

The ceramic mug toppled and thudded to the floor.

Chris's palm connected with Alan's jaw, shoving his face away, while he fought to get a leg on the floor.

Alan jammed his knee into Chris's gut.

A moan turned into a growl, and Chris shoved him off, rolling Alan onto the coffee table with a thud.

A jolt of pain shot through Alan's back.

"Are you guys for real?" Rebecca's voice rose above the clatter, coming out high and tight, as if she were on the verge of tears. Pushing, pulling, grappling for the upper hand, they probably appeared as little more than a mass of tangled limbs on the floor. "I guess I don't have to wait another month to have a kid in the house, after all."

Chris relented and pushed himself up to his hands and knees, then rocked onto his heels and stood. He scowled at

Alan then approached Rebecca.

Alan pushed himself up too, his back aching where it had hit the table.

Rebecca's bottom lip quivered. The tears would come any second. It didn't take much to set her off these days—a greeting card commercial, a video clip of a soldier's homecoming. Last week, she'd cried during the national anthem played before a hockey game.

Despite folded arms and a wrinkled brow that told him to stand back, Chris wrapped his arms around her, pulling her against his chest and kissing the top of her head. His voice was muffled by her hair. "I'm sorry, sweetheart."

Alan rubbed out the pain in his lower back and bent and straightened his left knee, causing it to pop and crack. "Good morning, Rebecca," he said, his greeting laced with sarcasm. He regretted his sharp tone when he caught sight of a tear trailing down her cheek.

She sniffed and wiped a hand across her eye but didn't answer.

"I'll be outside." He turned his gaze to Chris. "Shoveling," he spat, and then stomped to his bedroom.

He yanked off his t-shirt and pants and tugged on clean underwear, jeans, and a knit jersey.

Voices carried in from the hall. First Rebecca's, firm and reprimanding despite the tear he'd seen. Then Chris's, first contrite then more adamant. He couldn't make out the words.

After yanking on his jacket and shoving his hands into gloves, he grabbed a snow shovel outside the kitchen door and dug in.

The snow, powdery and feather light, slipped easily on and off the shovel. The peace of a fresh snowfall engulfed him. The absence of vehicles on the road made for a silent weekend morning, and the scent of burning wood filled him with a sense of warmth and nostalgia as he recalled his parents' wood-burning stove.

The scrape of the shovel against the concrete reminded him of the previous winter, when he and Jamie had removed a foot of snow from their driveway. Stranded at home for a day while they waited for the snowplow to reach their neighborhood, they'd made the most of their time together. They'd shoveled then played in the snow before thawing out in a hot shower and warming up with hot cocoa. Then they'd climbed into bed and played some more.

When they'd woke in the morning to discover the electricity, and therefore the heat, had gone out, they added two more blankets to the bed and kept each other warm until the afternoon.

For the millionth time, he contemplated what had gone wrong in their relationship. What was at the root of it? How could he fix it if he didn't know? His frustration mounting, he shoveled the walkway around the side of the house, his work quick and methodical. The snow tapered off, making his job both easier and more effective.

When he'd cleared the front steps and reached the driveway, the garage door hummed and opened, revealing Chris, fully dressed and sporting a bandage on his temple.

"Did I do that?" Alan flicked a hand toward Chris's forehead.

"Indirectly." He tightened a brown, wool scarf around his neck, failing to cover the scowl on his face. "I clipped the corner of the coffee table on the way to the floor." He stepped forward and the garage door lowered behind him. "We need to talk."

13

So Damn Lucky

Alan pushed the shovel toward the edge of the driveway, not wanting to deal with Chris, who stood near the garage door watching him. The peace he'd felt when he first started shoveling had faded, and now something tugged at his heart, as if just beyond his reach lay a solution. He'd engaged Jamie in a few stilted conversations, sent cards and small presents, even helped out financially with her mom's care, but things hadn't improved. Maybe the key had been there all along, the one that would facilitate a reunion with Jamie, land him a job, and make it all right again. His heart stirred, creating a little flip flop sensation.

"Alan?"

He ignored his fluttering heart and breathed deeply, ready to face the music.

Only Chris didn't appear angry now. His hair stood on end, tousled and matted. Circles darkened the skin beneath his eyes, and his shoulders sagged as he shoved his bare hands into the pockets of his fleece-lined, corduroy jacket. If that look had a name, "exhaustion" was it.

"I'm sorry about what happened in there." Chris titled his head toward the house. "My gripes with you are legitimate. I won't take that back. But, I provoked you. And I was inconsiderate. So . . . sorry." He rocked back on his heels, obviously relieved *that* was out of the way.

Alan let a grin slip, thinking the apology may have sprung from something other than brotherly love. "So, is that you talking or Rebecca?"

Chris grinned too and shrugged a shoulder. "The lines are kind of blurred. You know, that whole two become one thing?"

Yeah, well, he didn't know it so well anymore. "Gotcha." He leaned the shovel against the cinder block retaining wall on the opposite side of the drive. "I'm at least as much to blame." He shook his head and let the dejection cover him like a cloak. He might as well level with Chris. "I don't want to be here. You know that, right? I want to be in *my* house with *my* wife, not be the third wheel around here, freeloadin' and gettin' in the way."

"Well, it's kinda a relief to hear you say it. I mean, I've lived with you and Rebecca almost as long as I've lived with just Rebecca." He kicked the snow with the toe of his boot. "I didn't figure she'd get pregnant so quick, not that I'm not thrilled about it." He met Alan's gaze, obviously not wanting Alan to think he was anything less than overjoyed about this baby. "I just thought it would take a few more months or something. In the space of five months, we got married, bought a house, moved, got pregnant and took on a . . . houseguest."

Chris rubbed his fingers beneath his eyes and along the bridge of his nose. "And that's only the tip of the iceberg."

Alan wrinkled his nose. "What do you mean? You guys are great. I know it's been, like, huge changes—and I'm sorry for my part in it—but I don't know what it is. It's like, whatever comes, you've got it, and the two of you just get tighter and move on." He waved his hand in the air, suddenly tripping on an idea he hadn't given a moment's consideration.

He'd lived under the same roof as Chris and Rebecca for months. He observed their bowed heads before meals, the weekly treks to church, and the quiet moments at night when he sometimes discovered them curled up on the couch with rosaries dangling from their hands. He'd eaten in front of a wreath with purple and pink candles for a month before Christmas and sat curiously before a meager, meatless meal while staring at the dark smudges on their foreheads one recent Wednesday. Their faith was interwoven seamlessly into their love affair. For some reason, it hadn't occurred to him until now that perhaps faith had a bigger role in sustaining them than he'd ever considered. "What's going on below the surface?"

Chris closed his eyes. "Where to start . . ." He faltered, then went for the shovel and picked up where Alan had left off. The metal blade scraped over concrete.

The cogs and wheels in his brain still turning, Alan studied Chris for a moment . . . and then he got it. "So, you basically say your prayers and go to church, and it's like a get-outta-jail-free card, right?"

Chris jerked his head around. "Huh?"

"I'm just . . . I'm thinkin' here. I haven't been able to figure out what makes you guys tick. I mean, jeez, you didn't even . . ." He glanced around, self-conscious that someone might overhear although no one else was even outside. "You didn't have sex until after the wedding."

Chris averted his gaze, clearly uncomfortable with the direction Alan had taken.

"What do you get out of this? All the rules. The prayers and the customs and stuff." He recalled a stream of Hispanic people parading through the streets of Gettysburg last summer, a bunch of guys in robes in the front holding up a gold star-like candelabra or something and sending smoke into the air. What was *that* about?

Chris's gaze narrowed. "Are you sincere? Do you really want to know?"

Yes, he did. For the first time, he wanted to know why and what for and maybe even what it could do for him.

"Yeah, I am."

Something like surprise lit Chris's eyes, and after a moment's pause—was he praying?—he said, "It's not about me. It's about Him." He glanced up, where only a few stray flakes fell from the gray sky.

That he didn't get. Alan could learn rules; he could follow them. The relationship side of it, he didn't get. Frankly, didn't want. What he did want was some order, some resolution, some sense of up and down, right and wrong in his life. Direction, purpose. "So, you pray and go to church and it all, like, it makes sense? Everything's hunky-dory?"

"Hunky-dory?" Chris gave him an odd look. "Are you serious?"

Was he? "Yeah. I am. What's the payoff? Do this, this, and that and life gets easier? It makes some kinda blasted sense?"

Chris shook his head. "First off, do you pay any attention at all to what's going on in my life? My wife's super-pregnant and filled with irrational fears about being a mom, 'cause her own mom was AWOL. Her blood pressure creeps up at every doctor's visit. Oh, and the company I work for is tanking. Literally. As in beer production has practically stagnated because of equipment failure. Somehow, I got pulled into finding a solution, and they're talking about sending me somewhere they're either looking to buy or to do reconnaissance. I have no idea."

Alan kneaded his forehead. Okay, so he hadn't been paying enough attention to things, but still, just the fact that stuff hadn't been a big issue proved his point. They weathered these things like they were nothing. "Yeah, but—"

"Oh, no. You're going to get all of it." Chris stood the shovel up in the snow and leaned on it, slacking a hip. "My father-in-law hates me. Still. Barely speaks to Rebecca, but won't even tolerate my presence in the same room, not since the day he learned she was pregnant. And Rebecca's brother-in-law—this one you wouldn't know since I only found out last night—" His features relaxed, softened. "He was just diagnosed with a brain tumor."

"Abby's husband?" Rebecca's sister was a piece of work. Didn't the poor guy suffer enough?

"Yeah. Benign, thank God. But still." Chris picked up the shovel and started pushing snow toward the end of the driveway, his voice drifting over his shoulder. "He's going to have surgery. So, no, my faith isn't some kind of magic get-outta-jail-free card." Shovel loaded with snow, he stopped and said, "But it does mean I don't deal with all of this alone. And it—all suffering—has meaning and purpose." He resumed shoving the fluffy powder down the drive. "But I still think you're missing the point."

Alan caught up to him, snatching the shovel from his hands. "How so?"

"It's not what I can get out of it. If that's all you're after—some kind of prosperity gospel—don't waste your time."

Having no clue what a "prosperity gospel" was, Alan stood speechless while Chris trudged back to the garage, opened the door, and slipped inside.

14
If Only

Megan stared at the new spice rack nestled between a barrel of sourdough pretzels and the coffeemaker at the rear of Jamie's kitchen counter. Tarragon. Did she have tarragon? And more importantly, what *was* tarragon? Sounded like the hot guy with stringy hair from the *Lord of the Rings* movies Tim had made her sit through.

"Did you find it?" Jamie struggled to tie a bunch of parsley together with some kitchen string then huffed and dropped it into the stockpot on the stove.

Using her index finger, Megan traced a path along each row of spices. What was she doing here after work, trying to instruct Jamie in soup-making? She stocked her freezer with frozen meals, and her refrigerator and cupboards were almost as bare as Jamie's. She was the first to suggest eating out. It wasn't that she couldn't cook or even that she didn't enjoy it. It simply wasn't a skill she wanted to cultivate; it didn't quite fit her image as a cosmopolitan, carefree, career girl.

"Uh . . ." Megan scanned the tiny bottles again, her gaze roving over the labels twice before she realized they'd been alphabetized. "Got it!" She held up the small bottle of crushed green flakes, a smile of satisfaction lifting her spirits.

Jamie's mom used a paring knife to push her pile of sliced, peeled carrots to the edge of the cutting board. "Carrots are ready."

Petite with silver hair cut in a no-nonsense shingle bob,

wearing neither makeup nor jewelry, the kind-faced lady appeared to be close to seventy. That seemed about right given that Jamie had said her mom had been in her mid-forties when Jamie had been born. Jamie had set her up with a table tray so she could sit while she worked. Her recovery from the knee replacements had taken longer than expected due to an infection, but Megan guessed she'd be ready to be on her own again soon.

"So, Jamie, why the sudden urge to learn how to cook?" Megan measured the tarragon and dumped it into the stock pot. The warm aroma of chicken and herbs wafted on a swirling cloud of steam. If Jamie were interested in honing her cooking skills, wouldn't she have done it already? If providing healthy food for her and for Alan wasn't motivation enough, surely all the ribbing she took for her ineptitude in the kitchen was. Her lack of culinary skills was legendary.

Jamie wiped her hands on a dishcloth, sighed, and then grabbed the recipe card from the counter. "The recipe says this soup costs less than a dollar per serving." Jamie shook her head. "Do you know how much a bowl of soup at a fast casual restaurant costs?"

"Around five bucks." Megan dropped the sliced carrots into the pot and stirred, forcing more of the savory bouquet into the air. "Just think of the house you guys could've bought if you used your eating-out budget alone for a down payment."

Jamie, leaning against the counter in her jeans and long-sleeved t-shirt, shot her a withered glance. "Exactly. *That's* why I want to learn how to cook." She accepted the cutting board and knife from her mom and took them to the sink. "I'd like to keep us from going broke."

Jamie hadn't given her specifics, but Megan assumed she was financially strapped. Being on family leave caring for her recuperating mother would be challenge enough, but she presumed Jamie had lost Alan's income as well, little as it was lately.

"There's a simple solution," Jamie's mom said, pushing the tray table aside and smoothing her white polyester shirt. Her forehead knotted and a frown twisting her lips, she braced herself with a hand to each armrest and stood.

Megan darted a glance between Jamie and her mom, the dissension between them palpable.

"Invite your husband to come home." Her mom grabbed a wooden cane and angled toward the hall. "I'll be right back. Just going to take a bathroom break."

Jamie breathed out, and the irritation on her face dissolved. "Need any help?"

"No, thank you." Without turning back, her mom headed for the bathroom.

Once she'd moved out of earshot, Megan spoke. "I didn't think she cared for Alan much."

Jamie shrugged and tightened her low ponytail. "She didn't seem to, but lately . . ." She glanced toward the bathroom. "I think he's won her over."

"How's that possible when he's not even around?"

Jamie grinned. "Oh, believe me, he's done just enough to get on her good side."

Megan clapped the lid on the pot and leaned against the counter, curious as to how Alan, out of a job and kicked out by his wife, had been able to impress his formerly recalcitrant mother-in-law. "Such as?"

Jamie scooped up stray utensils from the counter and dropped them into the sink with a clatter. "Well, guess who came by to shovel us out when it snowed so Mom could get to her doctor's appointment?"

"Ah, now I see. Anything else?"

"Well," Jamie said, twisting the dish towel between her

hands. "He sold tickets for three Dave Matthews Band concerts this summer so I could buy Mom some medical equipment that wasn't covered by her insurance. I hated to ask for help because, honestly, I already felt kind of guilty about him paying the mortgage when he's not living here. And he'd lost his job. But I had no choice." Jamie's eyes watered as she scraped onion scraps into the trash. Megan guessed emotion rather than onion caused the tears.

Pushing off the counter, Megan strolled to Jamie and laid a hand on her shoulder. "So money's really the only reason you want to cook?"

Jamie glanced down, batting her eyes several times. "Megan," she whispered. "I do want Alan to come home. I miss him *so* much. I even miss the bits of beard stubble left in the bathroom sink and that stupid lock of hair that hangs over his eye."

Megan wrinkled her nose. "You miss *that*? I've wanted to snip that hair off about a thousand times."

Jamie chuckled, sniffed, and wiped her nose with the back of her hand. "There's a big part of me that wants to please him. I've been getting better at this, you know. The time-lapse videos and the step-by-step photo recipes—they help."

Megan nodded her encouragement. Anything that helped Jamie demystify recipes and learn unfamiliar cooking techniques had to be good. "So, why not just tell him? Tell him you want him to come home."

Jamie's jaw opened then slammed shut as her mom's cane tapped on the wooden floor, signaling her shuffling approach.

Laying her cane aside, her mom eased into the chair. "Don't clam up on my account. I'd like to know too. Why don't you ask your husband to come home?"

The stock pot clattered as steam rattled its lid, and

Megan quickly dialed the knob on the stove down to low.

Her spine stiff and her features tight, Jamie took a seat at the kitchen bar. She used her palm to sweep crumbs into a tiny pile in front of her. "You make it sound so simple."

Her mother stretched a hand out as if she wanted to comfort Jamie, but that was impossible from where she sat. "It *is* simple, honey. You're married. You took vows. That means you stick together and work it out, whatever it is."

Megan clenched her teeth. *Simple. Right.* Her parents had taken vows too, but that hadn't stopped her dad from leaving. That didn't make her mom willing to forgive. It was as if the second her brother Randy's body came home in that flag-draped casket, everything had tanked. Vows were only as sincere as the persons who made them. In her family, neither of her parents had intended to keep the promises they'd made.

"Mom, I don't know if he . . ." Jamie shook her head and brushed the pile of crumbs into her cupped palm. "We never talked about it."

"About what?" Jamie's mom stared intently at Jamie.

Megan began to feel like an intruder. Maybe they needed some mother/daughter time. She slipped the phone from her pocket and glanced at the time. She needed to be getting to Tim's place soon anyway. "Well, soup's good to go, so I should probably—"

"About getting married. About what it meant. About . . . forever." Jamie's voice quaked. "About babies."

As far as the other two women in the room were concerned, Megan may as well have drifted away on a cloud of steaming broth, invisible and unnoticed. She sighed and walked to the stove so she could peek at the soup's progress. Should she continue to blend into the background and wait out their conversation?

"Finally!" Jamie's mom smacked her palms against her polyester slacks. "It's the first time you've said it."

Interesting. Jamie's mom apparently hadn't heard her daughter's complaints about Alan and his sudden onset of baby fever.

"For a girl who spent half her childhood toting around baby dolls and her teenage years babysitting, your reluctance to have a baby . . . well, I don't get it, honey."

Neither did Megan, really. Alan may be a pain in the rear, but as a husband, he didn't seem half bad. Jamie may not be the domestic goddess that Chris's wife apparently was, but she'd be a good mom. In any case, her life sang love and stability whereas Megan's rasped alienation and aimlessness.

"Having a baby's a big deal," Jamie whined.

Megan lifted her brows, fairly certain they all knew babies were a big deal.

"And?" her mom prompted, arms folded across her chest.

A few beats of silence ticked by before the truth finally burst from Jamie. "And I don't want to do it alone. It scares me."

"And why would you be doing it alone?" Her mom's brow wrinkled. "You're married. Doesn't Alan want to be a father?"

Twisting the end of her ponytail, Jamie's voice softened. "He says he does." She lifted her chin and straightened her shoulders. "But he could change his mind. He only brought it up because Chris and Rebecca are having a baby. And, he doesn't have to *leave* to be gone."

Megan glanced between mother and daughter, their gazes locked on one another. Something more was going on here. Something Megan wasn't privy to.

Her mom's shoulders drooped, and she bent her head,

massaging her brow. "This is different, honey. Your dad did his best."

"He did? Really, Mom?" Jamie sprung from the stool and paced behind the counter bar. "He was there physically, but he resented me. He was never present emotionally. I wasn't on the agenda."

"What are you talking about, honey? Your daddy loved you."

Jamie shrugged, her stare hardening. "He never told me so. I know what happened, Mom. I can do the math. He was a longtime bachelor when you got together. He didn't want a baby. He probably didn't even want to be married, and then you got pregnant—"

"You don't know what you're talking about." Her voice came out angry, and her eyes shot daggers. Despite her age and small stature, Jamie's mom wouldn't be cowed by Jamie's insinuations.

Megan's stomach knotted, and her shoulders tensed. *Time to vamoose.* Their highly personal conversation had her backing out of the room. Megan's family had enough of its own dysfunction. She didn't need any more, thank you very much.

Being as unobtrusive as possible, Megan grabbed her things from the couch, murmured an excuse, and headed for the door.

Purse on her shoulder, Megan had one foot out the door as Megan's mom set her daughter straight.

"Your dad was depressed," she choked out. "He did the best he could. I promise."

Megan clicked the door shut, aborting Jamie's response. Depression, grief . . . they could eat a family alive from the inside out, devouring life and hope. Megan could attest to that.

She hoped Jamie and her mom could work things out for all their sakes. How long would it be before Alan gave up and started looking somewhere else? Or someone else went looking for him?

15
One Sweet World

March

The glimmer of morning sunlight peeking through the sheer curtains disappeared as Alan attempted to straighten his necktie for the third time. With a growl of frustration, he stomped to the light switch and flicked it on, then undid the tie again.

The mirror above the child-sized dresser didn't help. He had to bend his knees in order to see what he was doing. The room—his bedroom—had been transformed into a child's room, courtesy of a hand-me-down bedroom suite from Rebecca's sister, Abby, and her husband Joel. A few gouges and a half dozen dirty streaks marked the white wood that Chris intended to sand and repaint. The upside was Alan had a real bed to sleep in the last few weeks. It turned out to be less comfortable than the air mattress he'd been using, but at least it was off the floor.

Alan lifted the collar of his crisp, white shirt and crossed the wider end of the tie over the narrower one. As he threaded one end through the loop he'd created, Chris and Rebecca's voices traveled through the wall.

"Are you *sure* you're okay with this?" Chris asked for the umpteenth time.

For cripe's sake, man, she's sure.

"Because I'll just tell them I can't go. They can send Tom. His baby's not due for another four months."

Rebecca's voice, always softer and milder, sounded weary. "It's fine. I'm not due for almost two weeks. You're only going to be a couple hours away, and Alan's here.

First babies are known for being late anyway."

The woman didn't seem to do anything that could trigger labor. As per the midwife's orders, she'd been spending most of her time lying on her left side or sitting with her feet propped up, chugging water like a camel that'd just reached an oasis after weeks of wandering the desert. Alan didn't pay close attention, but it had something to do with her blood pressure going up.

This time the tie knotted perfectly, and he pulled on his seldom-worn gray suit coat, typically reserved for weddings and funerals. He'd considered canceling this job interview since the one he'd gone on last week had turned out so well. The guy had all but offered him the job on the spot. Just a few cursory calls to his references and Alan would be an account executive in outside business-to-business sales of digital payment solutions.

He lifted his chin, examining whether his knotted tie was centered and even. His thoughts drifted to when he'd gotten his last job, how Jamie had squealed with excitement and showered him with kisses and congratulations. Yeah, he was past ready for a replay of that pride shining in her eyes.

Today's interview was for an advertising sales position for a national media company. Alan preferred selling tangible assets with proven value rather than advertising, the first thing business owners cut when times were tough.

"Hey, you got a minute?" Chris poked his head in the door. Dressed in casual khaki pants and a Polo with the brewery logo over his left breast, he should've looked cool and confident. Instead, dark circles hung below his eyes and his hair stood on end in places, as if he hadn't slept in days. Rebecca complained she couldn't sleep well due to the baby's nocturnal activity. Must've been keeping Chris up too.

Alan glanced at his wristwatch. "I've got five, and then I've got to get to this interview. Shoot."

"I'm heading out. I'll be in Altoona most of the day. They wanted me there two days, but I'm going to see if these guys can stay late tonight and do it in one." He shifted his weight from foot to foot, tapping his fingertips together. "And then I can come back late tonight or worst case, first thing in the morning, by breakfast."

"Don't sweat it." Standing straight now and staring at his reflection—from the chest down, due to the kiddie-sized mirror—Alan adjusted his cuffs. "She's fine. I'll be around."

Chris nodded. "Yeah. You're right. I'm usually not so anxious. I don't know what's wrong with me."

Alan chuckled. "Uh, you're gonna be a dad soon. It's okay to be a little nervous. And excited. And scared."

"Yeah, I know. But I already gave it all to God, and that's usually enough." He stared at Alan as if that statement could possibly make sense to someone whose experience with God was next to nil. "Still can't seem to find any peace though. Can't say why." Chris backed out of the doorway.

Alan followed, thinking of the best route to take to get to the interview. Morning rush hour had ended, he could—

"Hey, good luck."

His gaze bounced to Chris, and he followed him into the living area. "Yeah, thanks. I think the one I interviewed for last week is in the bag. I figured it wouldn't hurt to go on this one though."

"It doesn't hurt to have another option," Chris said as he grabbed his overnight bag and set it alongside the door.

Rebecca waddled in from the kitchen and plopped onto the couch, water bottle in hand. "Knock 'em dead, Alan." A prayer book and a novel slid toward her as the cushion compressed under her weight.

He grinned. Yep. Another quiet day in the maternity ward. "Thanks. I'll catch you guys later."

As he opened the door, the sun emerged from behind the clouds, shining so brilliantly that Alan had to squint. He noticed as he descended the steps that the daffodils had emerged. Everything would be greening up. He'd have a new job. More income. And his mother-in-law would be going home.

And then he'd do whatever it took to make amends with Jamie. Nothing would stop him from getting back together with his wife.

***

Megan inched her MINI Cooper along the paved driveway beneath towering evergreens on either side. Their long, droopy limbs and soft, dark needles reminded her of a twisted cross between Tolkein's Ents and *Sesame Street*'s Snuffleupagus as they bobbed in the breeze. The porch of Tim's century-old, two-story home came into view, a pair of painted white rockers resting beneath a couple of empty hanging baskets.

She parked the car and leaned on the steering wheel, gaping up at the peeling cornflower blue paint on the gingerbread spanning the second-story eaves. *Good luck painting that.*

It all seemed surreal—Tim, a homeowner, living out here, going to church on Sundays and Wednesday evenings, hanging out with the Happy Hollister, as she'd taken to calling Tim's girlfriend. He'd even taken in a stray cat, of all things. A white, shaggy, cockeyed thing with one blue eye and one green eye. Lady Whiskers, he called it.

Her beer-pounding, dog-loving, sleep-till-noon big brother had become a teetotaling, church-going, cat person. All under the Hollister's watch. Megan hoped the Hollister had wriggled into her big girl panties this morning, because meet-the-kid-sister night was on.

A storm door trimmed in white swung open as she climbed the two steps of the stoop.

"Hey. Right on time. C'mon in." Tim, his feet bare beneath his gray track pants, ushered her inside with the wave of an arm. Lady Whiskers descended the stairs then rubbed her chin against the base of the newel post. She sat, staring at Megan as if she were the remnants of last week's stale kibble, and twitched her tail.

"How's my little lady?" Tim cooed at the feline, scratching under her chin.

Megan rolled her eyes and headed for the kitchen, where it smelled like red sauce and oregano. "I'm fine too. Thanks for asking." And she was supposed to endure this evening *sans* alcohol? If she shared Tim's faith, she might ask God to help her. As it was, she'd work on making this the shortest sibling meet-and-greet humanly possible.

As she turned the corner into a blue-and-white-checkered galley-style kitchen, a plump blonde with dancing blue eyes and a ridiculously huge smile squeezed from the booth in the breakfast nook. *The Hollister.*

She stretched a hand toward Megan, her smile growing impossibly wider. "I'm Holly. You must be Megan. I'm so happy to finally meet you." Megan detected the slightest drawl in the way she smothered the vowels in "you," rendering it closer to a "y'all."

"You too." Megan accepted the proffered hand, one lacking both nail polish and jewelry, and gave her a once-over. While not especially pretty or fashionable, she might be cute if she dropped twenty pounds and adopted a hairstyle that wasn't straight out of the 1980s—big bangs and a longish bob devoid of any layers. What had drawn Tim to her? She certainly wasn't part of the big-breasted, bubble-headed cohort of party girls from which he usually chose his girlfriends.

Stifling her lingering questions and pasting on a smile, Megan held the Hollister's hand firmly in hers and shook. "We finally meet." How was that for avoiding anything remotely complimentary?

"Tim's told me so much about you. I've been nagging him for months to get together with you." She elbowed Tim, who had come around to her side.

He squeezed her against him, no small feat considering her girth—

Megan's conscience pricked as Tim kissed the Hollister's forehead, his affection for her obvious. Her thoughts were more catty than those of Lady Whiskers, who proceeded to rub her chin against the Hollister's shin as she wound between the couple's legs, her crooked, nubby tail sweeping behind her.

Megan resolved to stifle her cruel impulses. For Tim's sake, she'd give the Hollister a fair shake and resist the urge to shake the stuffing out of the girl.

Tim moved to the refrigerator, opened the door, and scanned the contents. "What can I get you, Megan?"

"I guess a glass of chardonnay is out of the question?" She twisted her ring and glanced up at him without lifting her face. She couldn't help but crack a grin.

He met her amusement with disgust, slamming the refrigerator door so hard that a vinyl lunchbox perched on top fell to the faux tile floor.

Megan raised her hands in mock surrender. "Touchy, touchy. Iced tea or soda's fine. Whatever you've got."

Tim seared her with an angry look, but the Hollister brushed past him and pulled down a tall glass from the cupboard. "Ooh. I bought loose tea this afternoon and brewed it. I was hoping you'd like it. It's a fruit medley with apples, strawberries, blueberries, and pears." She flashed Megan a smile.

"Sounds fabulous!" Megan faked a return smile and then caught Tim's disapproving gaze. The second the Hollister's back turned, Megan stuck out her tongue.

Tim's glare lasted about two seconds before he broke into a smile, shaking his head and stepping out of the way.

The insipid dinner conversation detracted from the meal, which actually tasted quite good. Chicken parmesan and green beans with a homemade shoo fly pie for dessert. Apparently, the Hollister had some kitchen skills. She also appeared to wield some sort of magic since she had Tim helping in the kitchen as well.

After the table had been cleared and wiped clean, Tim motioned for the Hollister to sit beside him. He pushed out a third chair. "Megan, come sit with us."

From her vantage under the archway between the dining and living rooms, Megan glanced at the wall clock. Almost nine. She'd hoped to be making an escape by now. She'd endured almost two hours of the new-and-improved (bland and boring) Tim and played nice with the Hollister, whom she blamed for Tim's turn from holy terror to holy roller. If she left now, plenty of time remained for her to . . . whatever. Check out new Snapchat filters, clean out her makeup drawer, tweeze her eyebrows. Anything but more insufferable, uncomfortable conversation.

Tim's expectant eyes and stupid grin made it hard to bail just yet. The Hollister's face had that overeager puppy look too.

"Sure. I've got some stuff to do at home though. Can't stay long."

Tim clasped the Hollister's hand on the table, grinning. "This'll only take a few minutes." He didn't spare a glance for Megan.

"We wanted to get together sooner." The Hollister's eyes gleamed, and her cheeks flushed.

What was this?

Megan's gaze darted between the two of them, bubbly, giddy. *Oh, no.* She homed in on their hands. Tim's large hand engulfed the Hollister's smaller one, so she couldn't see if a ring hid beneath, but surely, she wouldn't have missed something so obvious. Besides, they'd only known each, what, six months?

"We told Mom this morning." Tim met Megan's gaze then glanced at the Hollister, whose smile stretched so wide even her molars were visible. "I've asked Holly to marry me—"

"And I said *yes!*" The Hollister's exclamation ended on a squeal.

The chicken parmesan soured in the pit of her stomach. Megan knew they expected congratulations. She knew her brother wanted her to share in his happiness. She knew these things, and yet she couldn't muster an ounce of joy. None. She was given a moment's reprieve by the kiss that now ensued.

Tim's hands framed the Hollister's face, partially buried in her hair. She gripped his arms, tugging him to her. Megan averted her eyes.

By the time they'd ended their lip-lock, Megan had summoned the expected expressions and words. She clapped her hands together and bounced in her seat. "Oh, that's fantastic! You guys . . ." She wagged a finger at them. "You really surprised me. I don't even see a ring."

"Oh." The Hollister glanced at her bare hand. "We're going to shop for one together." She gazed at Tim, animated pink hearts practically shooting from her eyes.

Tim blushed. He blushed? Tim didn't blush. "I was gonna wait until I had the ring, but I kinda jumped the gun. Couldn't wait to make her mine." He squeezed her against his side.

Megan forced another smile. What was the hurry? Pretty doubtful that the Hollister had other suitors lined up. Even less likely that she was pregnant. If she were such a Bible thumper, surely they weren't—oh. Maybe that was Tim's hurry? Either which way, she'd be having a long talk with Tim. But not now. She wasn't so heartless that she'd ruin their big announcement. Not to mention she wanted to talk to Tim in private, without the intrusion of the soon-to-be little missus.

If Megan stayed any longer, the evening would devolve into a discussion of bridesmaids' gowns, wedding colors, and honeymoon destinations. How could she extract herself from this little lovefest without seeming rude?

Megan coughed, moved her hand to her throat, and coughed again.

The lovebirds stared. Didn't they understand the international sign for choking? *What now?*

Her phone buzzed in her pocket. Perfect timing. *Thank you, whoever is interrupting me with a stupid text message.*

Megan smiled as the Hollister nudged a glass of water her way. "Thanks." As she lifted the glass to her mouth, she slipped the phone out and held it up. "Sorry. This could be important." *And it could be a notice that I've used fifty percent of my allotted cell minutes this month, but you'll never know.*

With a swipe to the phone, Megan caught the sender's name.

Alan?

She read and re-read his message, not sure what to make of it. *Thirsty? Crap day and I can't go back to Chris's yet.*

16

Save Me

Megan gripped the steering wheel as she swung into the shopping plaza parking lot, the car's headlights illuminating the small, bare trees lining the base of a large retaining wall. The big- box electronics store's brilliant yellow and blue sign sat at a jaunty angle above the large sliding glass doors. She circled once, searching for a spot from which she could see Alan exit.

She pulled in between a battered red KIA and a black Cadillac Escalade, watching as a couple of teenage boys exited and loped toward their vehicle, each with a bag in hand.

Within seconds of the engine clicking off, cold air seeped into the car, sending a chill up her spine and a sense of unease through her middle. For the hundredth time since she'd left Tim's, she questioned her judgment in agreeing to meet Alan for a few drinks.

She'd been so grateful for his interruption at Tim's that she'd have agreed to muck out stalls at one of the half-dozen Amish farms she'd passed. Beyond that, she liked Alan well enough, she'd grown weary of Jamie's failure to reconcile with him, and, boy, after facing the prospect of the Hollister as her sister-in-law, she could sure use a drink or two. Or five.

The fact that Alan had asked her to meet him here, however, set her on edge. He wanted her to drive. What did he have planned for the night? He could do as he pleased, but if he intended to get sloppy drunk and have her see him home—well, he'd better think again. After the

109

attitude he'd copped in November when he'd escorted her from the bar and practically forced her to take a ride with him instead of what's-his-name, she wouldn't be delivering him to wherever he called home these days. Had he mentioned Chris's place? No way was she dragging his sorry behind past the self-righteous stare of his super-pregnant sister-in-law.

A knock to her passenger side window startled Megan, and she jumped, her hand flying over her heart.

Alan stooped to peer through the window, a perturbed knot wrinkling his brow.

With the touch of a button, Megan unlocked the doors and Alan slid in, shoving a white plastic bag between his feet.

"What's that?"

"Oh," he said, giving the bag a shove with his foot, "baby monitor Rebecca wanted came in. She asked me to pick it up." He leaned back in the seat, his chest deflating on a deep sigh. Even in profile, Megan noticed the way his hair went every which way, the dullness of his eyes, and the slump of his shoulders. His head lolled to the side, and he caught her gaze. "Feel like getting wasted?"

She chafed at his expectations. When did she become the person he called when he wanted to be irresponsible and stupid?

If she could take tonight, jam it in a lockbox, and send it to the bottom of the ocean, she would. But her stubborn streak and a wee bit of self-respect wouldn't allow her to get stupid drunk tonight. It would just confirm everything Tim thought about her behind his slamming refrigerator door and holier-than-thou glare. "Thought I was the designated driver."

Alan's lips twisted. "I guess." He exhaled and leaned forward, slowly thudding his head against the dashboard.

"When did my life become so royally screwed up?"

Several smart aleck remarks came to mind, but Megan bit her lip. "What happened?"

He flopped back in his seat. "Let's go to Maury's, and I'll tell you all about it."

Maury's? A dive bar if there ever was one. Busted neon signs, cheap drinks, décor brought to you by the 1980s. At least she wouldn't run into anyone she knew there. "Maury's it is."

An hour and a half later, she'd heard Alan's sob story backwards and forwards, straight and slurred. His job interview had been a bust. When he checked his messages afterwards, he'd learned he hadn't even gotten a second interview on the job he thought was in the bag. He'd spent the remainder of the day in a second-run movie theater eating Jujubes and staring blankly at the screen, mulling over the many ways in which his life was a gargantuan disappointment.

Megan had three drinks to his seven. She glanced at the time on her phone and nodded to the bartender. She tilted her head toward Alan and made a slashing mark across her throat, signaling him to cut off her drunken companion. He lifted his chin in understanding.

"Know what I always wanted to do?" Alan twirled a swizzle stick in his glass, rattling the remaining ice. With his face half-shadowed in the dimly lit bar, his resemblance to Chris showed in the line of his jaw.

"Hmmm?" She was so ready for this night to be over. The sooner they left, the better. She was mostly okay to drive, wasn't she?

"Go on the road. I'd be a roadie for Dave Matthews. Save a helluva lot of money on tickets." His harsh laugh ended in a combination hiccup/cough.

"Speaking of the road, we're out of here." She stood and

slung her purse over her arm, hoping Alan would take the hint.

He must've understood because he stood and clumsily shoved in his stool. For a minute, he struggled with trying to unroll and button the sleeves of his dress shirt before Megan grabbed his forearm and turned him to the door.

Alan must've left every last ounce of self-control he possessed at the bar, because the moment the door swung shut behind them, he turned into a blubbering mess.

***

Tears dripped from his eyes to the oily gravel parking lot as Alan weaved toward Megan's car. He'd never felt so alone in all his life. It wasn't the first time he'd felt like a failure. A string of sales managers had beaten his shortcomings into him. He'd shrugged it off as best he could. He'd come into adulthood cocky and overconfident. He could afford to be knocked down a few pegs. Only now he'd slid from the bottom of the pegboard.

His foot twisted on a large rock, and he stumbled, slamming a hand out to steady himself on the cold, hard ground before he ruined his only suit. This was it. Rock bottom.

Megan's exasperated sigh pierced him. Why had he dragged her into this? If only he'd had somewhere else to go. Someone to turn to. *Jamie.* That's where he belonged. Just the tender look in her eyes and her fingertips on his cheek could dissipate whatever black cloud loomed over his head.

Eyes closed, he recalled the gentle touch of her hands, comforting and supportive as they kneaded his shoulders the day he'd learned the management position he'd been all but promised went to someone else.

With Megan's help, he settled in the car, again shoving the baby monitor out of the way. Thank God Chris was away and Rebecca would be asleep when he got back.

The car door slammed as Megan slid into the driver's seat. She jammed the key in the ignition and then hesitated, turning to him. Her eyes softened, and her lips turned up in a sad smile.

Even in the semi-darkness, the wide-set eyes stood out, framed by her porcelain skin and chestnut hair. He marveled at how pretty she was when she let down her guard. How and why had Chris resisted her all those years?

She reached a hand toward him and, after a moment's hesitation, laid it over his.

He wiped away a few more tears with his free hand, either too despondent or too hammered for embarrassment.

"It'll work out." She patted his hand. "There're other jobs."

Not another Jamie though. Couldn't replace his wife. Still, he appreciated Megan's attempt to make him feel better.

She leaned toward him, cocking her head, then shaking it gently.

"What?"

Megan ran a finger over his temple, wiped a tear, then used the back of her hand to stroke his cheek. "I don't know how I missed it for so long. How much you and your brother look alike."

Alan's heart clenched, an ache of loneliness radiating through his body. Jamie didn't want him anymore. Didn't love him. He couldn't take staying with his brother a day longer, seeing firsthand what he was missing. He knew touching Megan would be wrong, but the alcohol had clouded his feelings enough for the idea to wheedle its way in, and as Megan's fingers lingered on his face, to take root.

He knew she didn't feel anything for him. Nothing more than pity. And that amorous look was meant for Chris, not for him. Still, if she could take away this pain, this relentless loneliness, for now . . .

Megan stared, her glossy-eyed gaze flicking from one of his eyes to the other in the flash of a passing car's headlights, his attempt to follow it making him dizzy.

Drunk or not, he recognized the turning point before him. Nearly consumed by an insatiable desire to love and be loved, he considered lifting a hand to her face and kissing her. A dozen feelings tumbled through his mind and swirled amidst the broken pieces of his heart, then clashed against shame and regret. Without a thought, he threw up a wordless prayer to whatever god might listen. If the God Chris and Rebecca loved was everything they claimed by all the crazy things they did, then maybe He cared enough to throw Alan a bone. A crumb. Just one, itty bitty morsel of wisdom.

A sense of peace unlike any he'd known washed over him. Could've been the alcohol and emotion catching up with him. Maybe he was going to pass out. More difficult to explain away was the strong sense of purpose he had. That he was done slip-sliding through life. He may have slid into marriage, but he would not slip into adultery or divorce. He would choose.

Fidelity. That was his choice.

Megan tilted his chin toward her, her gray-green eyes mirroring the loneliness and loss that muddled his own thoughts a moment ago.

He sat back.

Her eyes glistened as she shrunk into her seat, and her hand fell to her lap.

Alan buried his face in his hands, trying to grind some sense into his inebriated brain with his fingertips. "I'm sorry." He managed to spare her a glance. He owed her that much. "Sorry about all this. Could you just drop me off at Chris and Rebecca's? It's—"

"I know where it is." Her voice was cool, and, if he wasn't mistaken, filled with the same disgust he now felt at what could've happened.

Silence was their companion on the ride back, the streets dark and somnolent. Alan felt both sick at heart and sick to the stomach. But he couldn't shake the memory of that fleeting moment of peace. How could he get more of that?

17
Steady As We Go

Alan jammed the key in the lock and pushed. The door didn't budge. He gave it an extra shove, and it swung open, the seal creaking.

Soft light spilled in from the living room along with the soft murmur of television voices.

He glanced at his watch. Well after midnight. *Rebecca's still awake?* He'd assumed she'd be in bed, and he wouldn't have to traipse by her in a semi-straight stagger.

With a push, the door shut behind him, and he turned the deadbolt. He slipped off his dress shoes and kicked them alongside Rebecca's Birkenstock sandals. The temperatures hadn't reached sandal-level yet, but her swollen feet no longer fit in her other shoes.

He raised his arm and sniffed his sleeve. A little cigarette smoke. A little cheap beer. None of Megan's perfume. Thank God. He breathed deeply to clear his head and rid himself of the lingering effects of the whiskey sours and his brush with temptation. With a clumsy tug, he straightened his wrinkled shirt as best he could, tucking it into his pants. Doing his best imitation of sober, he stepped evenly to the living room archway.

Rebecca paced the room, twisting her hands. She stopped and stared, her eyes wide and red, as if she'd been crying.

"Hey. What're you still doing up?" He flicked a glance at the round, wooden wall clock. "Try and get some sleep. Chris'll be here in like . . ." His brain couldn't process the simple math. "Like six or seven hours or something."

Her brow wrinkled, and a sad frown twisted her lips. "I think I'm in labor."

He blinked and refocused. "I'm sorry. What did you say?" Because she couldn't have said what he thought he just heard. She wasn't due for another week and a half or something. She couldn't be in labor. Not until Chris came back anyway.

"After you left I scrubbed down the kitchen cabinets. And then I started having contractions." Her eyes welled with tears.

Soothing emotional females was not his strong suit. Otherwise he'd be handling his *own* wife's meltdowns, not his brother's. "You probably just overdid it with the cleaning."

"No. I know what that feels like. All the Braxton-Hicks contractions."

The who?

"These are different. I've been timing them. They're three-and-a-half minutes apart."

He'd watched enough bad TV to know that if she was timing contractions, a baby was on its way. As if every trace of alcohol in his system had dried up, Alan's focus sharpened on Rebecca, her belly, and the impending arrival of his niece or nephew.

He held a hand out as if to stop her from panicking. If only he could stop the labor as easily. "Okay. We got this. Did you call Chris?"

A sob choked her answer. "I called him more than an hour ago. It's rolling to voicemail. I've left three messages." She pointed to the TV and a blotchy, angry, red-orange blob moving across the regional map, signifying a line of thunderstorms. "The storms are right over him. They're predicting hail and flash flooding. Someone's even spotted a funnel cloud."

"I'm sure Chris is fine." He needed to calm her. She sounded like she was about three weather events from full-on hyperventilation. "Let's, uh, let's time the next contraction." He slid his phone out of his pocket and searched the app store. There had to be an app for timing contractions, didn't there? He jabbed clumsily at the phone, trying to hit the tiny hyperlinks. His shoulders sagged in relief when finally he found one and waited for it to download.

Rebecca paced the room, breathing deeply. A little whimper escaped her lips.

"You okay?"

"That was another one."

Shoot. He'd missed it. "We'll get the next one." He held up his phone. "There's an app for that."

She sank into the couch, unimpressed.

"Can I, uh, make you some tea or something? And I'll give Chris a call myself. At least let him know we've got things under control here." A laugh bubbled in his throat, but he stifled it. He'd never felt less in control of anything in his life.

Without listening for her answer, he hustled to the kitchen. Fumbling with the handle, he grabbed the stainless steel tea kettle from the stove, filled it with water, and returned it to the burner. Where did she keep the tea bags? She'd been going on about raspberry tea this morning, and he hadn't paid her any attention. Maybe she stored it in one of those canisters along the countertop. He spun in that direction, teetering slightly.

Rebecca stood so close he almost smacked into her.

"Whoa. I didn't hear you. Water's on. You okay?"

She bit her lower lip and nodded. Her eyes welled with tears, and in seconds, they spilled from one eye and then the other. She swiped them away. "It's just . . . I'm so scared." A sob shook her shoulders.

He should comfort her. It was the right thing to do. But she was his brother's wife. And he wasn't the touchy-feely type. And then there was the practical matter of her huge belly.

Another sob shook her, and she gasped.

A pang of sympathy struck him. Of course she was scared. She'd never had a baby before, and she couldn't get in touch with Chris.

He opened his arms and pulled her to himself, sort of sideways so she could rest her head on his chest without the baby coming between them. This wasn't about his comfort. It was about hers.

"Shh." He stroked her hair and rubbed her back. "It'll be okay." What else was he supposed to say? What more could he do? "You, uh, you guys pray. Maybe now would be a good time."

Her head shook against him as she laughed. "You're right." She pulled away from him but held onto his hand. "Would you pray with me?"

He tapped his chest with his free hand. "Me?"

"You're the only one here." She grinned, her bleary eyes finally happy-looking, and pushed some stray hairs behind her ear.

"Uh, sure. Okay." He cleared his throat, trying to brace himself for the impending awkwardness.

She closed her eyes and squeezed his fingers. "Lord, I know you're here with us. And that I don't need to be afraid. Please give me the strength and courage to get through this. Bring Chris safely home to me." Her voice cracked. "Bless me and our baby and this delivery." Her fingers squeezed his again. "Thank you for Alan being here with me."

She was grateful for *him* being here? There were about a million and a half places he'd rather be. If he were to start praying—for real, with words—now would be a good time.

Her eyes widened, and she dropped his hand. She pursed her lips and moved both hands below her belly.

Apparently, this labor thing was still on.

"I-I think my, uh, my water just broke." She looked a little dazed, as if she didn't know what that meant or what to do.

He sure didn't. He glanced down, struggling to maintain his balance by widening his stance, but there was no puddle on the floor, and her stretchy black pants appeared dry. Of course, she had some big, blousy maternity top draped over most of her body. "You think?"

She nodded. "I'm sure. I'll go change and then, uh, I guess . . ."

"Do you need to go to the hospital?" *Please say no. Please say no.*

"I think so. Yeah." She turned and walked gingerly toward her bedroom.

Alan pivoted in the other direction, smacking a hand to his forehead and cursing under his breath. Was he sober enough to drive her? He hadn't taken his car tonight for a reason. Chris would kill him if he drove his pregnant wife to the hospital while under the influence.

The tea kettle whistled behind him. First a squeak, then a full-out, blaring whistle.

Maybe a cup of tea would help. He grabbed a couple of mugs from the cupboard and dropped one of Rebecca's raspberry tea bags into each. After pouring the water and sloshing some over the rims, he pushed them back on the counter to steep for a few minutes.

He padded down the hall and stood outside her bedroom door and listened for a second or two before knocking softly. "Rebecca? I'll call Abby. She can swing by and take us to the hospital. Where's your phone?"

The door swung open. He started and stepped back.

Rebecca wore the same top, but she'd changed into maternity jeans. She clutched an overnight bag in one hand. "No. Don't call Abby. She can't come."

"What do you mean? She'd want to come, right? I mean, especially since Chris is going to, uh, be a little late." Yeah, just a little late. He'd make it in time. He had to.

"They're sick. Her kids. They were throwing up all day. Every one of them. She sent Joel to a hotel. I don't want her anywhere near me and the baby."

"Oh." Made sense. Alan bobbed his head absently, as if the mere motion could enhance brain function. Now what? "I can call Mom. She'll be right here."

She shook her head. "In the morning. I don't want to wake her. Besides, I might be in labor for a really long time."

He pulled his cell phone from his back pocket and stared at the blank screen. There had to be someone. Other than him. "Okay. Um, I'll try Chris one more time. The tea's gonna get cold. We should drink it."

"Thanks. I forgot." She gasped and sucked in a breath, then leaned against the hallway wall, breathing heavily. Another contraction, he presumed. Her hand went to her swollen abdomen and then to her necklace. She fingered her wedding band where it hung from a gold chain. Along with her feet, her fingers had swollen, and with Chris's coaxing, she'd taken off the band a week ago amid a fit of tears.

Alan headed toward the kitchen, breathing deeply and glancing at his watch as he walked. When had he left the bar? And how many drinks was it altogether? Shoulders back and chin up, he walked a straight line with relative ease. He felt sober enough. Mostly. But this wasn't the kind of thing he wanted to take a chance on.

Only a few paces behind him, Rebecca reached the kitchen, steadying herself against the countertop.

He handed her the hot mug, hoping he looked more confident than he felt. "Here you go."

Her hand trembled as she took it, but she gave him a slight smile. "I'm so sorry about this, Alan. Chris should never have gone. We just didn't think—"

He held a hand up. "Whoa. Whoa. Did you just apologize for going into labor? Like you had any control over it?"

Rebecca bit her lower lip and glanced down. "I just mean . . . this is really uncomfortable for you, and you're stuck with me—"

"Hey. Forget it. I'm glad I'm here." But he wasn't. Not really. Sure, he wanted to help out, and he was glad she wasn't alone. But, man, did he wish it were someone else. Nevertheless, he'd do right by her, somehow. And never let Chris forget it.

The tea had cooled enough to sip. It burned his tongue on the way down, but he swallowed and worked up the nerve for what he had to tell her. She might change her mind about being thankful for his "help."

"I don't know if you noticed, but I didn't come home in my car tonight. I got a ride with a friend." He didn't have to mention Megan by name, did he? "On purpose. Because I wanted to have a few drinks and not worry."

Her brow wrinkled. "How much?"

He shrugged. "Maybe four beers. A couple of whiskey sours."

"Are you telling me you can't drive?" Her lip quivered and her voice cracked. "I don't want to . . ." The sobs broke through. "I don't want to have my baby alone in a dirty cab."

Okay. Now she was just becoming hysterical. Not that he could blame her. He was only two cars back on the crazy train.

"Who said anything about having the baby in a cab?" Did cabs even run out here? And besides, the point of the cab was to get to the hospital. Would she settle for Uber?

"Relax, Rebecca. We're not calling a cab." True enough, but who *were* they calling? Chris was AWOL. Abby was in quarantine. She'd nixed Mom. The list of people he could call for a ride in the middle of the night was pretty short.

Maybe if he hadn't just rejected Megan, he could ask her, but she never cared for Rebecca anyway. There was just one person. His heart ached at the thought.

Jamie.

Despite their differences, she loved Rebecca and wouldn't refuse her at a time like this. And he wanted to talk to her. Needed to, really. But after all this time, he hadn't anticipated their next meeting going like this. What would she think when he had to admit he only needed her help because he'd had too much to drink?

Rebecca sniffed and wiped her eyes, then toyed with her wedding band again.

He'd just suck it up and make the call. "I'm getting us a ride. It'll only take a few minutes."

She nodded and resumed pacing.

The phone rang for the third time as he stepped back into the hall.

"Hello?" Jamie's voice sounded groggy from sleep.

His heart lurched in his throat. The sound of her voice about did him in. The sudden realization of how deeply he'd missed her cleaved his heart with a thunderous ache. He swallowed both the pain and his pride in one monumental gulp. "Hey, it's me."

"Alan? Is something wrong?" Her voice morphed to

awake and alert.

"Not exactly. I'm with Rebecca, and she's in labor. Chris is out of town, and we can't get a hold of him. I need to get her to the hospital, but . . ."

"But what?"

His brain scrambled for a last-minute reprieve. Was there something else he could say? The shame weighed heavily on his chest. "I was out and I, uh, I had too much to drink. Probably shouldn't drive her—"

"You need me to take her to the hospital? Is that why you're calling?" Her voice scratched with urgency but not the irritation he'd anticipated.

Even so, he cringed and braced for it. "Yeah. Yeah, she—we—need a ride."

He waited for her to lambast him.

But, she didn't.

"Let me throw on some clothes. I'll be there in fifteen."

He let out a breath. "Thanks, Jamie." She was coming. Rebecca would be delivered safely to the hospital in minutes. And maybe a tête-à-tête with his wife had been delivered right into his lap.

"Tell her not to worry, okay? I'll be right there."

18

Lie in Our Graves

Her heart heavy, weighing her steps, Megan trudged through damp grass, stopping occasionally to stoop and aim her cell phone flashlight on a marker. A clouded sky prevented any moonlight from aiding her search. An owl hooted from somewhere in the distance. Tack this to the top of the list of creepiest things she'd ever done: wandering the cemetery alone at night.

She walked south another row, sure her brother's grave lay nearby. *There.* A small American flag stood motionless in the still air. That had to be it.

Megan brushed away a leaf and pushed the encroaching grass to the sides. How long since someone from the family had visited?

Randall Pettrey. Beneath his name, she touched the two dates. The space between them, the span of his life, pinched too narrow. Where there should've been summer luaus, hand-cut Christmas trees, hideous Father's Day neckties, and sandcastles at the beach, there lay only a couple inches of marble.

"I miss you."

Memories of the ways she'd tried to bury her grief burdened her heart and riddled her conscience, but she couldn't form the words or string together sentences. She felt ugly. Bone-deep ugly. Her cool reception of Tim's engagement. Her meanness toward Holly. The jealousy of their relationship. The emptiness and shame of her own life. Too many nights with men who meant nothing to her. Too many drinks that did nothing but delay the inevitable hollow ache where her soul used to be. The bitterness over Chris and her near-hatred of Rebecca. Even her previous indifference to Jamie's problems. For a half second after dropping Alan off, she'd considered driving straight into oncoming traffic.

Her sympathy for Alan had twisted into something else while they'd sat in that parking lot. His despondency and vulnerability had tempted her to use him as a temporary escape with barely a thought of her friend, his wife.

Warm tears rolled down her cheeks as she settled herself cross-legged in the damp grass. Wetness soaked through her jeans, but she didn't care. The tears came and then ebbed. Maybe Tim was right. Maybe she needed a change. Not rehab, but a fresh start. A new way of living and looking at the world. Her perspective had been skewed ever since Randy left them. She looked at the world through filmy lenses that distorted her perceptions and darkened her moods, leaving her a shrewish shadow of her former self.

Megan wasn't the first person to lose someone she loved tragically or unexpectedly. But nothing in her life had equipped her for such a loss. No faith. No consolation. No peace.

She and Tim had barely grieved their brother when the second loss struck: their parents' marriage. Neither of them had recovered from the divorce, which had left them feeling perpetually homeless. Well, maybe that wasn't true anymore. To her annoyance, Tim seemed almost whole lately, like he had it all together.

Scattered drops of rain pattered against the headstone, and Megan studied a droplet as it traced the "U" in U.S. Army, puddling in the bottom of the letter before dribbling into the soil below.

Eleanor, Randy's fiancée. She'd had it all together too. So

much so that Megan used to love hanging out with her. How had she coped? Megan had lost touch with her a month or two after the funeral, when the phone calls had grown too painful. She'd even stopped checking the memorial website Eleanor had created. Did she keep it updated? It'd been more than a year since Megan had visited it.

She brought up the website on her phone. Pulling her sleeve over her palm, she wiped the dampness from the screen. Her jaw clenched at the sight of Randy in uniform and the collage of photos of him and Eleanor. She clicked under the blog, surprised to find an entry so recent—last month, the anniversary of their engagement.

She skimmed the first couple of paragraphs in which Eleanor recalled Randy's proposal, scrolled down to an image of a hand-written letter and enlarged it. Apparently, Eleanor put it all out there. All the grief, the love, the personal stuff. It felt like an invasion of privacy to Megan, but it must've comforted Eleanor. Had Megan stymied her own healing by keeping it all bottled up?

The image was a snippet of the letter with only the midsection visible. Megan smiled at the familiar ink strokes, printed capital letters with t-bars slanting down.

"If my service means anything, it means there are things worth fighting and dying for. That this life is worth it. That if someday I come home in a box, it won't be the end of all things. Grieve me for a time. Then take courage and live this beautiful life you've been given. Love again. Live without regrets. Trust in God as you always have."

As the rain droplets grew in size and frequency, Megan glossed over the final paragraphs in the entry, Eleanor's words. It sounded like she was grappling with the possibility of a new relationship while trying to honor Randy's memory and his wishes. She re-read Randy's mention of God. Had he had a come-to-Jesus moment in Afghanistan? She recalled Eleanor always wearing a cross necklace and bowing her head before meals, but they'd never discussed her faith. Maybe they should've.

Raindrops pattered onto the grass, the marker, and Megan's head, first gently, then harder, building to a downpour within a minute. Goosebumps rose on her neck as a cold trail of rainwater slithered beneath her collar and down her back, causing her to shiver. Megan stood and raised her chin, blinking into the murky darkness. Let the rain wash it all away. The loss, the ugliness, every regret.

When the sun rose, so would she, her heart a smidge lighter than it'd been when she'd wandered into the graveyard. She had amends to make. With her parents. With Tim and Holly. With Jamie and Alan and Chris and Rebecca. Maybe even with God. Who knew?

And Eleanor. She'd reach out to Eleanor.

19
Time Bomb

With few cars on the road, they'd get to the hospital in fifteen minutes, barring red lights or—God forbid—an accident. Alan rode shotgun, his gaze aimed out the window at the passing orchards, cornfields, and city streets. He clenched and unclenched the hand pressed against his restless leg.

Rebecca shifted in the back seat, then leaned back, a little moan escaping her. Next second, she sucked in a deep breath and blew it out her mouth.

Jamie glanced in the rearview mirror. "Rain's supposed to stop by morning and the next few days will be warm and sunny. Perfect for bringing home a baby, right?

Alan couldn't think past the impending birth let alone carry on a conversation, so Jamie's gentle reassurances and efforts to distract Rebecca with small talk impressed him. Cool as a cucumber; the kind of person you could count on in a crisis.

He found himself sucking in another breath with Rebecca, realized it, and shaking his head, blew it out, forcing several strands of hair into the air. *Get a grip, man.*

The car rolled up in front of the giant, glass hospital doors. Amid the dark night and quiet streets, the bright lights seemed out of place. A large fleur-de-lis illuminated on the side of the main building hovered over the words Trinity Hospital.

Alan popped open the door and helped Rebecca out of

the back seat. Maybe it was the angle she used to hoist her herself up, but if he didn't know better, he'd swear she'd shoved a basketball—or two—up her shirt. The kid couldn't possibly have grown in the last half hour—could it?

The glass doors slid open, and he took Rebecca's bag and led her with a hand to her back. He motioned her toward the empty lobby and ducked back out. Did Jamie intend to stay or go? He really wished she'd stay, both for his sake and Rebecca's.

The passenger side window glided down, and he rested his hands on the door, leaning down so they could speak face to face. "Are you gonna stay? I think Rebecca needs a—"

"I'll stay." She held his gaze for a moment, somber. Was she disappointed in his behavior again? They hadn't had a moment alone for him to explain. Not that he had a good excuse.

She rummaged through the cup holders and shifted in her seat, searching the car floor. "Shoot. I left without my phone." Sighing, she shifted the car into drive. "I'll park the car."

He lifted his hands and stepped back as the car pulled away.

"Alan?"

Chiding himself for ignoring Rebecca's needs, he spun and rushed through the doors. "C'mon. Let's get you up to maternity."

Adrenalin pumped through his system as he escorted her down the hall. This was it. She was going to have this baby, and Chris was still MIA.

He shuffled Rebecca past a bulletin board filled with newborn photos. Babies in metal buckets, terra cotta pots, and wicker baskets. Babies' bare bottoms, wrinkly fingers, and long-lashed eyes.

The décor on this floor resembled a hotel more than a hospital. Photos of families hung from the walls of the carpeted hall and the wooden handrail made the floor seem warmer, less sterile. It helped put him at ease. At least a little.

Rebecca checked in, and a nurse escorted them to a room.

He hung back at the doorway, not sure whether to enter or wait in the hall. Did she need privacy? Did she want to be alone? Or did she need him there for moral support? Because that's about all he could offer. He hadn't even witnessed a litter of puppies being born let alone a human being. If he happened on one of those reality shows about labor and delivery, he zipped on by, either to sports or cable shows a smidge shy of being porn. The stuff Mom wouldn't approve of him watching.

The creeping shame reminded him he was not his brother. Though he was older, he wasn't half the man Chris had turned out to be. He had no business being here witnessing a birth. Chris was responsible, respectable, and faithful. He'd make a great father. As good as their own.

Maybe it was a blessing in disguise, Jamie not wanting children. Seriously. Neither one of them were model parent material. But they could change that, couldn't they?

"Mr. Reynolds?"

Hearing his name, his attention returned to the room. Rebecca had disappeared behind the privacy curtain, so he stepped forward. "Uh, yeah?"

"My name's Crystal. I'll be here for"—she glanced at the wall clock—"the next four hours." Her short dark hair highlighted a round, open face. Alan put her age around late 30s. "Your sister-in-law explained that you're here in your brother's place. Is that correct?"

"Yeah. Yeah, but he'll be here soon, I'm sure." He would,

right? His hand slid to the phone in his pocket. Maybe he ought to call again.

"Okay." She glanced at the curtain then padded toward him, keeping her voice low. "I get the sense she could use the support. Your job is to be encouraging." Her instructions were plain and the hands to her hips communicated her authority. "She'll take care of the rest. And we'll help her."

He nodded. Supportive and encouraging. He could do that.

"Rebecca's in active labor, but she's probably got a while to go. I'm going to help her into the tub, see how she does there. You might as well make yourself at home." She gestured toward the wooden set of drawers, boxy chair, and closet area.

"Thank you."

Not knowing what else to do, he sunk into the chair. Where was Jamie? Would she come to the room or wait in the family area?

Low voices and the sound of rushing water came from the adjoining bath. A splash and then a groan, and a minute later Crystal returned, her smile affirming that the situation was under control.

"She's good for now. Buzz if you need anything." She grabbed a couple papers and sterile wrappers from the bedside tray and slipped out the door.

He sighed and let his head roll back in the seat. He had a thing or two to say to this kid once it arrived. Coming in the middle of the night when Dad's missing and Uncle Alan's drunk? Not a good move.

His phone buzzed in his pocket, and he hurried to pull it out. *Please let it be Chris.* He glanced at the caller ID. *Yes.*

"Dude, where have you been?" He stood and ran a hand through his hair.

"What's going on?" Worry sounded in his voice. "I've got like six messages between you and Rebecca, and she's not picking up. Is she okay? Is the baby all right?"

"We're at the hospital. She's in labor."

"What?"

Alan jerked the phone away from his ear a second too late.

"You're kidding me." He swore. "I'm on my way now."

"When you gonna be here? Cause her water broke about an hour ago, and my experience with delivery is limited to Chinese food and pizza."

"Uh . . . an hour and a half? I don't know. It's raining hard. It's dark."

"Where have you been? Not a great idea to go off the grid when your wife is nine months pregnant."

"Joyriding through the Pennsylvania countryside, what do you think?" Chris's irritation barely masked his worry. "By the time I got out of there it was almost eleven o'clock. The car blew a tire, damaged the rim, and I had to get a tow—which took forever. Can't get a rental car in the middle of the night there, so the guy helped me with the rim. Then I couldn't find the car charger for my phone. It was a total screw-up. I just got a charge now."

"Yeah, well, explain it to your wife." Alan plopped back in the chair, relieved Chris was on his way and in communication, even if he was an hour or more away.

"You think I wanted this to happen?" He could hear the irritation, maybe even a little panic, in Chris's voice.

"No, of course not."

The sound of rushing water stopped, replaced by the humming of the tub jets.

Alan lowered his voice. "Relax. She's okay. She's in the tub. I'm here. It's all good."

"How far apart are the contractions? You said her water

broke. Is she dilated?"

Dilated? "How should I know? And what do her eyes have to do with—" He caught his mistake too late. Chris wasn't asking about her eyes, he—

"Her cervix, you idiot. Is her cervix dilated?"

Alan squeezed his eyes shut, embarrassment heating his neck, and considered Chris's question. The midwife hadn't even been in to examine Rebecca. "All I know is I came home, and she said her contractions were, like, three minutes apart. Then her water broke, and we came to the hospital."

Maybe later he'd explain that Jamie drove them and why, but not now.

Chris cursed. "I want to be there, Alan. For Rebecca. To see my baby born." Alan didn't miss the crack in his voice.

"You'll be here. She's in good hands. Just drive safely, okay?"

"Okay. . . okay." The windshield wipers whirred in the background and the sound of rain hitting the car's roof grew louder. "Tell her I love her. I'm sorry. So sorry. And I'll be there as soon as humanly possible."

Alan smiled. Too bad he wasn't more like Chris. He was a good man, through and through. They shared the same genes though, so maybe there was hope for Alan yet. "I will."

"Alan?" Rebecca's voice came from the bathroom.

"Hey, I'm gonna go. Drive safe. She's in, uh—" He walked out the door and peeked at the number affixed to the wall. "She's in room 404."

He ended the call with Chris and stepped one foot into the bathroom. Sterile in contrast to the birthing room, it contained only a commode, sink, and tub. The fluorescent lights were off, but light came through the blinds on the single-pane window opposite the tub. No privacy curtain.

Rebecca must be naked; she was in a bathtub, right? Was she covered? He kept his head angled toward the window. "Hey, you need something?"

"Some water? The nurse said she'd bring ice water."

Alan turned away from the bathroom, his gaze darting around the birthing suite. There it was, on the table—a giant plastic mug filled with water. He grabbed it and returned to the bathroom entrance.

"I've got the water. Are you. . . are you decent?"

Rebecca let out a sharp laugh. "I'm in the tub. What do you think?"

That's what he was afraid of. Rebecca was beautiful, pregnant or not, but she was Chris's wife. Totally off-limits. Not goin' there.

"Um, okay." He kept his gaze trained to the ceiling as he walked in and lowered the mug onto the tub ledge, nearly missing it and almost dropping the mug into the bath. It must have looked humorous, but Rebecca didn't laugh. In fact, she didn't say anything.

That she'd lost both her modesty and her sense of humor made him think this baby wasn't going to wait too much longer.

If you exist, God, if you're even there, get my brother here pronto.

It was the closest he'd come to a real prayer—ever, but desperation had pushed him to it.

"Chris called. Said to tell you he loves you. He had car trouble and had sort of lost his phone charger, but he's on his way. He'll be here."

"Soon?" There was no missing the pleading in her voice.

"Fast as he can."

Rebecca half-whimpered, half-groaned through what he presumed was another contraction. "Is Jamie still here?"

Great question. "I think so, but she doesn't have her

phone, and—"

"Never mind. I don't want you gone looking for her." She'd nixed his possible escape. "Please stay, Alan."

He blew out a breath. How could he say no?

Alan grabbed a chair from the room, its legs squawking as he dragged it across the floor. He spun it around so that it was close to but facing away from the tub and sat. "Do you want to talk? Or should I just keep quiet?"

The water sloshed in the tub. "You can talk. I'm listening. But don't expect answers. It's getting hard to . . . to focus for too long."

He nodded. "Okay. What should I talk about?" What did he and Rebecca have in common anyway, besides Chris? That was it. Chris. "I know. You want to hear about Chris when he was a kid?"

"Sure."

He struggled to recall something, anything funny from when they were kids. Or even interesting. His mind drew a blank.

"Let me think." Maybe if he just started talking, something would come to him. "Okay. When he was nine, Chris took his bike out determined to ride it down MacKenzie Hill. It's that big one, behind the cul-de-sac off of Mom and Dad's street. You know the one?"

"Mm-hmm." More water sloshing.

"So, it's just a dirt trail the neighborhood kids made, but he pushed his bike up there, and when he gets to the top, it starts raining." He glanced out the window, where rainwater splattered against the glass as it bounced off the narrow ledge. "So, he's already up there. Nothing to do but come down. Me and three other kids, we're at the bottom, goading him on. So, he lets out this, I don't know, Tarzan call or something, and starts down." He paused, wondering if she were still paying attention or if she just wanted to hear the sound of someone's voice.

"I'm listening."

He grinned, remembering the day, some of the tension in his shoulders easing. "He's bumping along, coming all way down, and at the very end, he hits this mound and careens to the side into this flash-flood puddle or something and wipes out." He recreated the descent and landing with his hands, not sure if Rebecca was watching.

"Oh, your mom probably wanted to kill him." Her voice sounded tired but light. She was probably between contractions.

"Oh, yeah." Alan laughed, picturing Chris. "He looked like the creature from the Black Lagoon or something. The muck's dripping off him, but he pulls his bike into the garage, and he's got a smile on his face a mile wide 'cuz the whole neighborhood knows he killed MacKenzie Hill."

Rebecca groaned behind him, louder and longer than he'd heard before. "Alan, I think I want to get out. Can you . . . can you get the nurse?"

"Yeah, uh, sure." He stood, pushed his chair to the side and buzzed the nurse from the button connected to the bed.

Within minutes, the nurse arrived, and he waited behind the pulled curtain until Rebecca was out of the tub and situated in her bed. Or so he thought. When the nurse slid the curtain back, Rebecca was on all fours atop the mattress, clad only in the hospital gown.

His eyes must've bugged out because the nurse snickered.

"She's having a lot of back labor. Sometimes that's a more comfortable position."

Alan lowered his voice. "Is she going to have the baby, like *now*?" Suddenly all the tension returned to his shoulders, and a heavy weight pressed against his chest.

The nurse fussed with the machine they'd called the fetal monitor. "It's hard to say, but I wouldn't be surprised if she's ready to push soon. Maybe in the next hour?"

"Push? She can't. My brother's on his way. He'll be here in an hour or so. Less now."

The nurse smiled. "It's her first. It may take some time. But the baby will come when the baby's ready to come. Not sooner and not later, whether Daddy's here or not." She brushed past him and out the door.

20

American Baby

Raking a hand through his hair, Alan turned his back on Rebecca, who re-situated herself on the bed for the thousandth time. He was so not cut out for this job. Chris had months to prepare. He went to birthing classes with Rebecca and listened to her read aloud from all kinds of pregnancy books.

"Alan?"

Shoot. Could he slink out the door and hide? No, he couldn't. He wouldn't. "Yeah, Rebecca?"

"In my . . . in my bag, there's a sock with a tennis ball in it."

A what?

"Can you get it? If you press it into my back, it'll relieve some of the pressure."

"O-Okay." He pulled open the bureau drawer and dug around inside her bag, pushing aside a baby book, notepad, and slippers until he found the sock-ball.

For the next half hour or more, he pressed that ball as hard as he could into her lower back, trying desperately to keep his eyes from all the bare skin unintentionally exposed due to the flimsy hospital gown. Where had Jamie gone? She didn't have her phone. He should've told her to find them, not hang out in some waiting area.

Normal speech seemed beyond Rebecca now as her glazed eyes either squeezed shut or bounced about the room, lingering for a few moments on this or that—mainly the crucifix that hung on the wall opposite the bed—as she

139

steadied her breathing. She tried three different positions—leaning against the wall, over the side of bed, hands and knees, growing more agitated with each passing minute until she groaned and pleaded. "I can't do this anymore."

He swung the sock ball in circles, glancing around the room as if something there could ease her pain. What should he do? Maybe she needed some pain medication. Just knock her out for the rest of it. But she'd told him she didn't want any of that stuff, that she wanted to do things naturally.

Leaning with her arms braced against the bed, she broke into a sob. "I can't . . . I can't take any more pain."

"All right, all right." His heart knocking in his chest, Alan buzzed the nurse again.

In a few minutes, Crystal backed through the door, pulling a large metal cart with an array of instruments on it covered in plastic. Another nurse and the midwife followed.

What was this? He backed up, knocking into a tray table on wheels. She said she couldn't handle any more. Were they going to drug her? Or do a c-section or what? "What's going on?"

Rebecca shifted on the bed, groaning again.

"Sounds like this baby's ready to come out." The midwife, an athletic-looking, fifty-something woman, gave him a chipper grin.

He lifted his chin in acknowledgment, as if he'd arrived at the same conclusion. It was blasted three in the morning or something, and Chris hadn't arrived. She was happy about this?

The midwife spoke to Rebecca as the nurses maneuvered the cart to the foot of her bed, removing the plastic cover and arranging things just so. With a hand to the remote, the midwife adjusted the bed and then switched on a bright light aimed between Rebecca's legs as she lay in a semi-reclined position.

Her knees were bent, and the nurse helped her scoot to the edge of the bed.

Oh, no. Oh, God, no.

He felt the blood drain from his face, his head growing light and his chest growing tight. *I shouldn't be here. I shouldn't be here. Chris. Where on earth is Chris?*

This was it.

"Do you feel like you need to push yet, Rebecca?" the midwife asked.

Rebecca let out a throaty groan like he'd never heard from her before. "Yes. Please. I need to push."

The second nurse who had come in pulled what looked like a metal and plastic bassinet on wheels into position. Still grappling with the fact Rebecca was gonna pop this kid out now, Alan approached. "My brother, her husband. H-he's not here yet. How long is it gonna take?" He glanced at the midwife, who looked to be in baby-catching position. "How long does the pushing go on?"

The nurse smiled and opened her mouth to reply when the door swung open again.

Chris stood motionless in the doorway, his gaze darting around the room until it landed on Rebecca. He strode forward, his brow creased with worry. Water dripped from his hair, and his shirt was soaked through. The smell of fresh rainwater preceded him.

As if someone had loosened the pressure valve in Alan's chest, he relaxed. "Hey." He thrust his arm out, grabbing Chris's. "You're just in time."

Chris turned to him, obviously not having even noticed him before. He let out a deep sigh. "Thank God."

Thank God. He'd prayed Chris would make it in time.

And he had. Barely, but still. Had God heard his prayer?

"They just brought all this stuff in." Alan gestured to the table and the bassinet. "She's ready to push."

Chris placed a hand on Alan's shoulder and met his gaze, his eyes tired but steady. "Thank you."

Two words, but heartfelt ones. Chris must've been sick with worry. That Alan had been there with Rebecca had probably been his only comfort, pathetic as it was.

Rebecca caught sight of him. "Chris. You're here!" Her exclamation ended on a sob that quickly turned into a near-growl.

"Deep breath." The nurse counseled Rebecca from the side of the bed where she held back Rebecca's leg. "Then push through the contraction."

Alan winced at the strain evident in Rebecca's moan.

Chris rushed to her side.

The midwife directed him to dry off and wash up in the bathroom while Rebecca rested between contractions.

In seconds, he was back at Rebecca's side, holding her hand and covering her head with kisses while she cried and murmured to him.

"Ready for the next one, Rebecca?" The midwife scooted closer on her wheeled stool. As if they were cast in a well-rehearsed play, they each took their positions, even Chris.

Grateful he was no longer needed, Alan slipped from the room. In the hallway, he breathed deeply and leaned against the wall. The growling wail from inside the room signified the next contraction. More murmurs followed along with Chris's reassurances. "You're doin' great, honey. We're gonna hold our baby real soon."

Alan padded down the hall, running a hand through his hair and over the stubble on his cheeks. Would Jamie be in the waiting room? Probably not. She must've gone home. He'd be stuck here, but that was okay. He'd hang around for a while after the birth, then have Chris give him a lift home.

He stepped into the waiting room. Empty. No rain jacket or sign anyone had recently occupied the space. Not even an abandoned coffee cup or water bottle. Alan's heart sunk.

With a sigh, he sat and slouched back on the stiff, padded chair, the emotions and anxiety of the night combined with the late—or rather, early—hour catching up with him. He rested his head on the seatback and stared at the ceiling tiles. The soft yellow glow of a tabletop lamp relaxed him. Maybe he could switch off the light and rest his eyes for a few minutes.

A loud clap sounded from the hall, as if someone had dropped a tray.

Alan jerked to attention, an ache starting in his neck. He rubbed it away and stood, pacing the small room. Had Rebecca had the baby yet? By the looks of things when he'd left, that baby should've shot out of her within minutes if not seconds. But what did he know? Would he be able to hear anything from here? Any guttural wails heralding the delivery? The first cries of his little niece or nephew?

His heart swelled at the thought. They'd been looking forward to this day for months. He'd been privy to Rebecca's growing belly and the steady influx of baby gear into their home, yet it hadn't felt real until now, with the baby's arrival imminent.

Any minute now, his younger brother's life would be irrevocably changed. His responsibilities would increase. His house would be filled with stinky diapers, a gazillion toys, cheesy fish-shaped crackers, and . . . his throat thickened. Love. Their little home would be filled with love and drool-filled smiles, baby belly laughs, and sloppy kid kisses. His eyes stung, and he blinked away tears.

He shook his head. Had he contracted baby fever? He couldn't blame the alcohol. That had worn off. Before envy could creep in and steal the joy he felt for Chris, Rebecca, his parents, and himself, he forced his mind in another direction. His gaze caught on the reading material left on the table, the glossy magazine covers dull in the dim light.

With a flick of his hand, he spread the magazines. Chick stuff. Some boring medical magazine. Two books teetered on the edge of the table, one a kid's book with anthropomorphic horses on the cover and the other a plain, navy hardcover. He flipped it over and around. A Bible.

Shifting his weight to a hip, he thumbed through the pages. *Never read one of these before.*

The corridor was quiet now, and Alan poked his head around the corner. No sign of Chris. No baby's cry. He gripped the Bible and returned to his seat. What did he have to lose? He'd already lost his job. His home. His pride. His wife.

The thin pages slid through his fingers as his eyes scanned the chapters. Might as well start at the beginning. He skimmed a few pages until his gaze snagged on familiar words: "And the two shall become one flesh." He read the few preceding paragraphs and the ones after. This was one of the passages read at Chris and Rebecca's wedding.

If it were true, that would explain why it felt like his heart was cleaved in two every time he thought of Jamie and their life together. How much had he damaged their relationship tonight? He'd chosen her over temptation; he'd honored his vows. But he'd been stupid. Again. At the worst possible time. He'd had to rely on her to bail him out, and he didn't know—

"Alan?"

Jamie stood in the entryway, a purse slung over her

shoulder and a paperboard cup in one hand. A hint of hazelnut drifted his way. She'd twisted her hair into a knot in the back as she often did at night. He could picture her on their couch with her head resting on the arm, a long t-shirt riding up her bare thighs and her feet propped on a throw pillow. Yep, heart wrenched in two.

She dropped her purse onto a chair. "I saw Chris run by. Did she have the baby yet?" Her eyes were concerned, eager . . . happy?

Alan stood, returning the Bible to the table. "Chris made it in time. She's pushing now. I have no idea how long that takes. Longer for the first baby?"

"I'm so glad. He'd be so upset if he'd missed it." She clasped her hands together around her cup and gave a little squeal. "Ooh, I can't wait to hold the baby. Do you think it's a boy or a girl?"

Alan blinked. She was excited about the baby now? "Uh, I don't know. They think it's a girl, so I'll go with girl."

Jamie's smiled faded. She gave him a tender look, and her eyes grew teary.

His heart pounded in his chest, aching to beat in time with its mate. "It might be a little while."

A tall, thin, late middle-aged man with thick glasses ambled into the room, offering an uncomfortable smile and holding up his cup of coffee as if toasting them. He fell into an empty chair and stretched out his legs. *So much for privacy.*

Alan looked to Jamie and nodded toward the hall. "You wanna . . . you wanna go somewhere and talk?"

21

Dive In

Alan held the door open and motioned Jamie into the chapel ahead of him. The stained glass behind the altar appeared almost black in the night, but Alan imagined the west-facing windows shone beautifully at sunset, casting an array of colors across the tiled floor. He'd done his best to avoid hospitals and hadn't stepped foot into a hospital chapel until now, but this one wasn't so bad.

Jamie had suggested it, and he'd agreed. Neither of them could come up with another viable, private option on the hospital campus at this time of night.

He glanced at the crucifix suspended from the ceiling then the alcove filled with glimmering candles encased in red glass. Churches and places of worship generally left him feeling like a fish out of water. His memory flashed to a pair of teenage girls in Justin Bieber t-shirts that he'd spotted at the Dave Matthews Band concert on Thanksgiving weekend. He'd hummed to himself, "Which of these things doesn't belong?"

Jamie strode to the front of the mini-church and sat in the second pew.

After a moment's hesitation, he followed, recalling how Chris and Rebecca dropped to one knee before entering a pew but not knowing if that was necessary. He slid along the bare, wooden seat until their thighs were mere inches apart. Sitting alongside her might be better than facing off. In some small way, it reminded him they were on the same team. Or at least they should be.

Jamie twisted her hands in her lap, taking in the altar and casting him anxious glances. Why the nerves?

He hadn't let himself think about it before, but what if she'd had it with him? What if she wanted a divorce? What would he do? The thought of going through life without her made him sick, and he grappled with what to say and how to start.

Jamie attempted to cross one leg over the other, the shallow depth of the pew thwarting her. She twisted and tried to do the same with the other leg, only to give up and swivel her body in his direction. "I'm so glad Chris made it on time."

He hoped she was easing into a more intimate conversation, not avoiding it. They'd been separated too long, and darned if he was going to spend their precious minutes together talking about anyone but the two of them. If she thought for a second they were going to—

"I envy them, you know." She said it matter-of-factly, no shame and no bitterness. "These last months, I've gotten to know Rebecca better. She's sweet." Jamie smiled and pushed a lock of hair behind her ear, looking pretty sweet herself.

Alan rubbed his hands up and down his thighs, eager to get to the meat of the conversation. "Yeah. She's great. So is Chris. I don't know what I would've done without them since, well, since—"

"Since I kicked you out." Her gaze dropped, her expression chagrined. "Y'know, it's not just all this stuff with the baby coming. I've paid attention to them, Chris and Rebecca. The closer they get to one another, the more they turn out, the more their love just spills out all over the place." She splayed her hands in front of her. "It doesn't make sense to me, Alan. But I want that. I want it so badly."

She twisted toward him, taking his hands in hers. "I want it with you."

He swallowed, the emotion in his chest swelling, but remained unsure of what to say.

"Everything about their relationship is intentional. I know they're not perfect, and neither is their marriage, but I can't imagine either of them ever go to bed wondering if the other loves them."

No, not likely. Not if the amount of time he spent sleeping with his head buried under his pillow was any indication.

"Or wondering if it was all a mistake."

His spine went rigid. That little addendum to her thought caught him off guard. "You think getting married was a mistake?"

The silence lingered, and she bit her lip. "I don't know why we even got married, do you?"

He shook his head. "Not really. Seemed like we should." He moved his hands over hers and squeezed them. "But I want to stay married. I do."

"I feel like we're at such a disadvantage. They talked about marriage, kids, values, and faith, all of it before they even got engaged. What did we talk about? Who did the dishes more often or whose checking account was the rent coming out of this month."

He shrugged. True enough. Disadvantage or not, he wasn't letting his marriage slip through his fingers. "We'll work harder then. We'll make up for it."

His confidence brought a glimmer to her eyes. Was that hope or was she going to cry? "I'm not sure I'm sorry I asked you to leave even though I've missed you like crazy. Missed waking up with you. Missed sitting across the table from you."

Guaranteed, he'd missed her more. He lifted her hand to

his lips and kissed her knuckles. "Why not?"

"Because we might not be here now. I've been carrying around some stuff, some hurt from my relationship with my dad." She glanced at the ceiling, as if she'd find the right words there. "According to my mom, I misunderstood. I thought that he'd never wanted to be a dad. That that's why he half ignored me. I didn't know he suffered from depression for years."

He nodded, not sure yet where she was headed with this.

"I was afraid that would happen with you. If we had a baby, you'd regret it, that you'd lose interest. I thought . . ." She worried her bottom lip. "I thought you were just going along with the flow. A baby was the next thing to tick off the list."

Was he? Maybe a little. But he did want babies with her. And he was all about living purposefully now. Intentionally. "I want a baby because I love you. I want to share that with you." He shook his head. "I'm not going anywhere."

A sob caught in her throat, and she placed her hand over her mouth. "I didn't give you enough credit. I'm sorry. You're a good man, Alan. A good husband. I made you out to be a selfish child, but I was the one who was afraid."

"Nah. I've had some growing up to do." Still did.

"You were here for Rebecca. You stuck with her even though I know it must've been the last place you wanted to be. You did what had to be done. Because you love her and Chris. Because it was the right thing to do." She bit her lips together, her eyes teary but filled with admiration. "You put their needs above your own."

He squirmed, uncomfortable with the praise. What kind of jerk would he have to be to abandon his sister-in-law while she was in labor? And Jamie didn't know about before, how he'd gone out and gotten drunk after his job interviews tanked. He had to tell her. "Don't give me too much credit. If you could've read my mind, or if you knew what happened before—"

"So we both have some stuff to work on. I want to work on it together." Her chin lifted; her chest expanded. "I know now—tonight only confirmed it—that I can count on you to be the man I need."

With all the fluttering and pounding his heart was doing, he was relieved to be in a hospital. Between the baby getting ready to make its grand entrance and Jamie putting all her faith in him, going all in, cardiac arrest seemed like a real possibility.

She wanted this. Him. Their marriage. "'Til death do us part?"

She giggled. "Yeah. Let's give it a whirl."

The anvil that had been parked on his chest for months lifted. He thought he had an inkling of what Rebecca would feel when she finally delivered that baby—relief, gratitude, utter joy. Was this what they called "grace"?

***

Only silence slipped under the door to Room 404, so Alan rapped three times and waited.

A few seconds later, Chris pulled open the door. He smiled despite the circles beneath his eyes and the fact that his hair had dried in a funky-looking, spiky style. Stubble dotted his chin and cheeks. And yet the joy on his face blew Alan away.

"C'mon in. I didn't know if you stuck around. I should've come out to see, but—"

"Nah. You were busy." Alan stepped through the entranceway and stretched his arm out for Jamie to enter ahead of him.

Chris's eyes widened. "Jamie. Wow. Um, I didn't know

you were here. It's good to see you."

Her cheeks reddened, and her gaze slid to her feet for a half second. "You too. Congratulations, Dad."

Chris's smile widened, and he ran a hand through his hair, shaking his head. "Yeah. Thanks. Almost didn't make it. But . . ." He stopped and glanced heavenward. "I'm so grateful I did." His voice thickened, and he cleared his throat. "Well, come meet your nephew."

"It's a boy?" A son. Alan tamped down the envy creeping into his heart. There was hardly any room for it anyway with the joy already filling it to near capacity.

"Yep. Seven pounds, six ounces. Uh, nineteen and a half inches." Chris ambled toward the center of the room.

Rebecca reclined in the bed, her hair pulled back from her face, and her eyes tired, but a relaxed, happy glow about her that wasn't there a couple of hours earlier. In her arms, she held a little bundle wrapped in a white blanket with blue and pink stripes, and a hat to match.

Alan rounded the bed until he could glimpse the little guy. A pudgy, reddish face with no visible neck poked above the blanket. The baby blinked slowly.

"Uncle Alan and Aunt Jamie are here, sweetie." Rebecca acted as if it were the most normal thing in the world for him and Jamie to arrive together despite the fact they'd been apart for months. At the sound of her voice, the baby's eyes moved in her direction, and a tiny fist found its way out of the blanket.

Jamie grabbed hold of Alan's sleeve and leaned forward. "Oh, Rebecca. He's beautiful." She glanced at Chris then back at the baby. "He has Chris's eyes and chin."

Chris stood at the foot of the bed, his hands in his pockets. "You think so?"

"Yeah, she's right." Alan took a closer look. Close-set blue eyes. Oval chin. Would he have Chris's dimples? It was hard to tell with the knit cap, but—"Not much hair, huh?"

Rebecca giggled. "I think we've got a little baldie."

"Does he have a name yet?" Jamie looked to Rebecca.

Chris rounded the opposite side of the bed. "Sebastian Christopher Reynolds."

"I love it. It suits him." Jamie's eyes sparkled, and the smile never left her face. Who was this woman, all gaga over a newborn baby? Couldn't be his wife, could it? Could she be ready for one of her own?

"Do you want to hold him?" Rebecca stared at Alan, lifting the baby a little in his direction.

He looked to Jamie. "Uh, sure." He'd never held a newborn before.

Jamie nudged his elbow. "Go wash your hands."

"Oh. Okay." When he returned a minute later, Chris stood behind the empty rocking chair, cooing at the baby in his arms. Alan sat, shifting until he felt comfortable. Didn't want to drop the little guy.

Chris placed Sebastian in his open arms. His body was swaddled from the neck down. He did have a neck, didn't he? It certainly wasn't visible. His lips puckered then relaxed, and his paper-thin eyelids lay closed.

A rush of emotion choked Alan. "Hey, buddy."

22

Hello Again

Jamie proceeded through the revolving door, stopping in the semi-circular drop-off/pick-up area outside the hospital entrance.

Alan followed, grinning as their eyes met.

She held his gaze for only second before her glance dropped shyly to her purse.

His heart swelled and lifted, every emotion, every sensation mimicking a newfound love, a secret crush unexpectedly, delightedly requited. He couldn't keep the smile from his face. The joy he'd felt holding his nephew had been indescribable. Every fine hair, every inch of blotchy skin, and those little blue eyes. He marveled at the perfection. If he hadn't been so genuinely happy for Chris and Rebecca, he'd have been jealous. Only the affection he'd felt for that swaddled newborn, who smelled of life and hope and . . . and *blessing*, it was so big it had crowded out every base emotion.

Alan stepped toward Jamie, touching her elbow. He wanted to hold a child of his own, a ruddy-faced son or a bow-lipped daughter. But even more he craved holding his wife in their bed, and for the first time in months, the hope of that didn't seem as empty as his stomach currently did.

Jamie blinked up at him, her tired eyes filled with affection. For him or for the bundle of joy they'd just left behind, he wasn't certain, but he was fairly sure she'd been as affected as he was.

"Want to get breakfast?" Later, the lack of sleep would catch up with him, but right now, he'd keep her close as long as he could. "We could hit a diner. I mean, I don't have my car, so whatever you—"

"I have a better idea." She gave him a coy smile and looped her arm through his.

A thrill shot through him at her nearness.

"How would you like to be the first diner at Chez Jamie?" She squeezed his arm.

"Uh, hmmm . . . is that someplace new?" She couldn't cook her way out of a doggy bag. What was she getting at?

She giggled—*giggled*. "Yeah. Since you, uh, pay the bills, I thought you'd like to dine on the house. I can have breakfast ready in twenty."

His eyes bugged. "*You're* cooking breakfast?" He knew his reaction might be met with disdain, but he couldn't stop it.

She nodded, biting her lower lip. "Sure am. How do breakfast burritos and fruit salad sound?"

His stomached growled in answer. "Great, but how did you—when did you—?"

She shrugged. "Mom gave me some lessons. Megan helped me out a bit, and I watched some how-to videos." She leaned in, nestling her head against him as they headed in what he presumed was the direction of her parked car. "I'm no great chef, but I think you'll be surprised how far I've come." She lifted her chin and gave him a smug grin. "Haven't burned or ruined a meal in two months."

Two months? The promise of a decent meal cooked in his kitchen was alluring enough, but it wilted like day-old lettuce in comparison to the fact that she'd been working for months at this. He knew it wasn't necessarily for him. She could have lots of reasons for learning to cook. But the way she'd flirted and dangled this surprise before him with pride shining in her bright blue eyes told him it had at least something to do with pleasing him, which meant she cared about him—still.

"Consider me ready to be wowed." Before he could overthink it and change his mind, he stopped and wrapped his free arm around her, pulling her into a hug. His heart kicked to life and, paradoxically, his soul calmed. Home. More than where they were headed, a place he'd missed more than he ever would've guessed, *this* was his home.

The arms of this red-headed beauty were his starting and ending point. Much like his parents' home when he was a child, it's where he turned for safety and security, the one place he knew complete and absolute acceptance. Her arms were the launching pad for every astounding success and the solace in every crushing defeat. More than any other place, here is where he could most fully be himself, where he could laugh, cry, or simply be.

In the past, he'd taken that to mean indulging his own whims without thought to repercussion, but now he knew that it was more about being who he was meant to be, the best version of himself. His family, Jamie, was the starting point and testing ground for every upgrade. Alan 2.0 would be the man his wife needed first and foremost, and somehow things would fall into place. They had to.

Jamie sighed deeply and leaned into him, letting him support her entirely. In a small way, he sensed she was giving herself to him again. With no hesitation, no obvious fear or doubt, she'd just revealed her willingness to cling to him, no matter what had gone before.

"Let's go." He squeezed her once, savoring the feel of her in his arms once again. "I'm starved. I hope Chez Jamie serves super-sized portions."

She pulled out of his arms and dug the car keys from her coat pocket. "Don't worry. The chef knows your legendary appetite." The twinkle in her eye and the wry quirk of her lips made him wonder if she was thinking of more than food. He dismissed the thought, determined not to get ahead of himself.

He bowed and ushered her forward, making a sweeping motion with his arm. "Lead the way."

A half hour later, as Jamie pulled into their driveway, sunlight streamed over the rooftops and between the trees. Car engines came to life as people rushed from their houses to their cars with work bags and coffee in hand.

Alan stared at their brick ranch house. It wasn't anything special. It was everything special. Behind its walls they laughed, they cried, they argued, and they made love. He'd missed it. "Your mom home?"

Jamie opened the door, walked around to the front of the car, and waited for him. "We moved Mom back home on Wednesday."

A thrill shot through him, but he steeled his expression. "Oh. Sorry I missed saying goodbye."

She snorted and halfheartedly punched him in the side. "You are not. Thanks for trying though." He'd missed her smile, her laughter.

A grin broke free. "Can't say I'm too disappointed. We haven't been alone together in what feels like forever." Alone together. How long had it been since Chris and Rebecca had been alone together without him getting in the way? He filed the thought away, for now.

He glanced at Mrs. Simpson's silver Toyota and nodded his head in its direction. "Mrs. Simpson saw me standing shirtless out here the morning you kicked me out."

Jamie smirked. "I know. She told me."

"Yeah?" He recalled the twitchy look Mrs. Simpson had given him. "She thinks I'm hot?"

The sound of Jamie's laughter made him forget how tired he should be. "On the contrary, she thought you must be cold. She asked me what you were doing outside without a shirt or a jacket."

He chuckled, surprised that he could laugh at something that had brought him so much pain.

"*I* think you're hot though." Jamie came closer, looping her fingers through the belt loops of his slacks. The same ones he'd been wearing since yesterday's disastrous interview.

"Speaking of hot . . ." He could go in so many directions with this. "I believe I was promised a hot breakfast."

"A hot breakfast you will get," Jamie said, heading for the front door. She stopped short, her key in the lock, and kissed his cheek, searing the skin beneath a day's growth of beard. "Welcome to Chez Jamie."

Inside, Alan's shoulders—his whole body—relaxed. *Home.* Be it ever so humble and all that jazz. Later, he'd soak it all in, but right now he needed a shave, a shower, a bottle of mouthwash, and some clean clothes.

Twenty minutes later, he returned to the kitchen invigorated by the shower and this potential new lease on married life. Onions and peppers sizzled in melted butter on the stovetop, and the smell of coffee brewing lured him deeper into the kitchen, where Jamie cocked a hip against the kitchen counter.

He moved closer to her, toe to toe. "I'm gonna get you one of those 'Kiss the Cook' aprons."

Her eyes twinkled, and the corner of her lips turned up in a flirty smile. "I don't need one of those to get a kiss, do I?"

Definitely not.

She reached up and crossed her wrists behind his neck, her body bumping his. "If you're waiting for an engraved invitation, I think I've got one of those." She loosed a hand and waved it in front of him, wiggling her ring finger encircled by her white gold wedding band.

His pulse sped. Alan was different now, and this kiss should be different too. Not a cursory kiss given as one of them ran out the door. Not an obligatory part of foreplay. Not one of the many sloppy, drunken kisses they'd shared. Or the rote kisses that had become routine between them.

What he poured into this kiss needed to be just right—the perfect melding of passion and purpose. The kiss of a man who was ready, willing, and able—scratch that, *eager*—to be a husband and a father, with a clear understanding of the sacrifices those roles demanded.

Jamie must've sensed his earnestness because the smile fell from her face and the gaze of her blue eyes locked onto his. Her chin lifted on a breath, and he slid his hand along her jaw and cupped the back of her head. Her eyes closed, and her implicit trust spurred him on.

His hand sunk into her hair, and he inched closer, their bodies touching, his lips so close to hers that the hitch in her breath fanned over his jaw. "And the two . . ." He feathered a kiss over her lips. ". . . shall become . . ." Another kiss, her lips soft and pliant beneath his.

One more shallow breath.

One more moment of exquisite tension.

He reached his other hand around her waist. ". . . one." His lips met hers, and he poured every ounce of love from his heart into hers, a soul-deep fusion. In a blissful moment no longer than the flutter of a heartbeat, he lost track of where he ended and she began.

23
Mercy

April

Megan avoided staring over the oak-stained coffee table at Chris by fixing her gaze on a painting of whom she assumed must be Jesus and his mother. She angled her head to the side. Yep. The halos were a dead giveaway. Intimate and pious. So unlike the scene between Megan and her mom two weeks ago.

Despite the dread that had pooled in her belly, Megan had initiated a long heart-to-heart talk with her mom. After forcing out two admissions and one apology with no more response than a deriding stare and a clenched jaw from her mom, Megan had been tempted to abandon her reconciliation tour before it'd gotten underway.

Chris sat still, his sleeping baby pressed against his chest. One arm cradled the baby's bottom covered in a yellow terrycloth sleeper while the other hand rubbed circles on the baby's back. He lifted his chin as his eyes darted toward the kitchen. "Rebecca will be right back."

Megan nodded from her seat on the blue-gray upholstered chair opposite the couch and gave a polite smile. She'd bet given the chance, he'd bolt, but he was stuck. Trapped by the infant snoozing against him. His shoulders had the same uncomfortable slant as her dad's last week when he'd excused himself from their conversation twice to tend to his wife's obnoxious purse dog.

Although Megan's palms had turned cool and clammy as

she rehashed her string of *I'm sorrys*, Dad had mellowed more quickly than Mom. He'd listened to her series of *mea culpas*, asked a couple of excruciating questions, lobbed some excoriating criticism, and then squeezed her in the same style side hug he'd perfected on her brothers.

"How's it going?" Chris's question snapped both Megan and the infant to attention. The baby's arm jerked, and Chris steadied him with a palm to the little guy's back.

"Good." She crossed her legs, smoothed her plum slacks, and bobbed her foot nervously. "I won't take much of your time." She'd nearly gotten these apology appointments down to a science. No aching chest or churning stomach today, only some general nervousness.

After a satisfactory visit with Mom and an encouraging détente with Dad, she'd invited Tim and the Hollister—uh, Holly—to her apartment for dessert. She'd learned to manage the anxiety-induced symptoms these conversations created, knowing that the long-term peace outweighed the short-term misery.

She faced a giddy-in-love Tim and Holly over a piece of pineapple upside-down cake. "I'm sorry I've not been very welcoming to you, Holly, and so hostile to your . . ." She swirled her hand in the air, searching for the right words. "Your life changes, Tim."

Tim shoved back his chair, its legs stuttering against the floor, and in two strides stood at her side, pulling her from her chair and hugging her. Hard. Megan didn't even fight the tears. And when Tim used the opportunity to talk to her about Jesus, she didn't flinch. He hadn't sold her on the concept—not completely—but for the first time, she didn't resent the effort.

She turned her thoughts and attention back to Chris, who gave her a nervous smile and glanced toward the kitchen. The baby stirred, and Chris nuzzled him, murmuring softly.

She'd yet to get a good look at the little guy although Jamie had shared some pictures. He must be three weeks old now. "What's his name again?" Alan or Jamie must've told her, but she couldn't recall.

"Sebastian. Sebastian Christopher."

Sebastian squirmed, and Chris repositioned him, turning him around so she could get a good look. Wide blue eyes and a few wisps of dark hair. He yawned, his little body shuddering.

"He's beautiful." Delicate skin, button nose, and innocent blue eyes that wheedled their way into Megan's decidedly non-maternal heart.

Sebastian twisted toward his dad, his little fist clenching. His tiny, pink mouth opened and closed, and he rubbed his face against Chris's t-shirt.

Megan had thought she'd exorcised all her feelings for Chris over the past several weeks, all the old infatuation. One look at him cuddling his baby, and it came rushing back. There wasn't anything sexier than a man with a baby. That little ball of pudgy perfection held by muscular arms against a sturdy chest. Did Rebecca have any idea how lucky she was?

When his mom entered the room, Sebastian lifted his head and started rubbing furiously against Chris.

"Sorry to make you wait, Megan." Rebecca had a little post-partum paunch, but otherwise you'd never guess she'd given birth only a few weeks ago. Her eyes appeared tired, but her voice seemed perky enough. "I'd been waiting all day for that callback from the restaurant. We want to have a little reception after Sebastian's baptism next week."

Chris glanced at Rebecca. "Hey, he's rooting. I think he's hungry."

"Again? Didn't I just feed him?" She ran a hand over Chris's shoulder as she passed behind the couch and then sat next to him, squinting at the clock on their entertainment system. "I guess it's been almost two hours."

At the sound of her nearby voice, Sebastian broke into a howl, and Chris handed him over.

She took the baby, settled him on her lap and undid something under her shirt.

Every movement between them was so familiar and easy. Utterly free. Megan quashed an unexpected surge of envy.

Rebecca's hand hesitated at the hem of her shirt, and she cast Megan a wary glance. Probably deciding whether to take care of her baby's needs in private and risk leaving her husband alone any longer with a reputed man-eater who harbored a long-term near-obsession for him.

Megan bit back a grin. "Go ahead and feed him. I don't mind."

Rebecca acknowledged her with a stare then proceeded to move the baby into position at her breast and helped him latch on.

Chris's loving gaze fell on mother and baby, and he gently stroked the back of Sebastian's head with his fingertips. They'd been married almost a year, and they still acted like lovesick pups despite the fact they spent day and night wiping a baby's bottom and losing sleep.

Megan sighed and averted her eyes. This is what Alan and Jamie craved. And if the ache in her chest was any indication, deep in her heart, she wanted it someday too.

"Megan," Rebecca said as she patted the baby's rump. "Would you like something to eat or drink?" She turned to Chris. "Would you grab that plate of banana bread on the counter?"

"Sure." He pinched Sebastian's toes and kissed Rebecca's

head before he rose, his tired gaze so filled with devotion.

"I'm fine. Really." Too late. Chris had shuffled off to the kitchen. Megan had forgotten that besides being Little Miss Perfect, Rebecca was some kind of baking goddess as well. Her recently-revived conscience pricked her, and she reminded herself to be kind, not catty.

Chris returned, munching and holding a piece of the sweet-smelling bread in one hand and a small plate of it in the other. He set the plate on the table and grabbed a small piece and fed it to Rebecca since her hands were occupied holding the baby in position.

The scene reminded her of dinner with Alan and Jamie earlier in the week—Jamie had cooked! Alan's eyes smoldered as Jamie offered him a bite of her dessert. Megan smirked, wondering if they could wait until she left to enact their plans to start a family. She schooled her thoughts and, heart pounding, cleared her throat, drawing their attention. "I value both of your friendships. That's why I need to be straight with you." Megan had prepared herself to be lambasted by one or both of them riled by justified anger. Instead, she left their house, heart overflowing, their relationship strengthened rather than diminished.

Megan squared her shoulders and steeled her courage. Time to get this last one over with. She sucked in a breath, willed the butterflies in her stomach to settle, and prayed?—yes, prayed—she'd get the words right.

"I'll keep this short. I have an opportunity to make a new start, and I'll be moving next month. But before I do that, I've been making the rounds, offering some apologies. I've already done that with my family, and I saw Alan and Jamie the other night." She gave them a tight smile, trying to ease the tension. "You two are last on my last."

Rebecca's brow furrowed. "Us?" She glanced at Chris,

whose expression didn't betray whether he felt an apology was warranted or not. "You don't need to apologize to us."

Megan shifted in her seat, twisting her hands. "Oh, I do." She sighed. These apologies were the most humbling thing she'd ever done, but with each one, her spirit felt lighter, the relief fanning the flicker of hope that had ignited in her heart in the cold, dark cemetery.

"I've not respected your feelings, Chris, or, uh, lack thereof. And I didn't respect your relationship with Rebecca either." There was more, of course, but nothing more she'd say out loud. Maybe, someday, if she could accept what Tim had been telling her about Jesus, she'd confess it to Him.

Chris glanced at Rebecca. He opened his mouth and closed it, not seeming to know what the appropriate response might be. Finally, he nodded.

She shifted her focus to Rebecca, whose brow wrinkled in confusion. "Rebecca, I'm sorry for any unkind thing I have may have done or said to you or about you. It's obvious to anyone who spends five minutes with the two of you that you belong together."

There. She got it out. She braced for Rebecca's reaction. She could demand to know how she'd failed to respect their relationship or what she'd said about Rebecca and to whom.

After a moment's pause, her expression unruffled, Rebecca simply said, "All's forgiven."

Megan forced herself to meet each of their gazes. "Thank you." The squeaky crack in her voice surprised her, but then everything about these past few weeks surprised her. Tim called it "grace." Megan figured she was teetering on an emotional breakdown.

"Um, so, where are you moving?" Rebecca's face didn't betray any emotion. Did she forgive Megan or had she said so only to shorten the visit?

"Down south. My brother, uh, not Tim . . . Randy, who died." She flicked a glance at Chris, who might not remember Randy but would remember his death. "His fiancée—former fiancée—she invited me."

By the end of Megan's stumbling reply, Rebecca hardly seemed as if she were listening. She scooped her now-sleeping baby from her lap and glanced at Megan, a gleam in her eyes. Megan didn't understand the look until Rebecca stepped carefully around the coffee table and lowered the baby, placing him gently in Megan's arms.

"Oh." Megan raised her elbow, ensuring she was supporting the baby's neck and head. His mouth opened as if he were still suckling, his eyelids fluttering in sleep. The warmth of his little body soaked through her cotton shirt, melting her hardened heart in a puddle that sopped up every last trace of resentment she harbored for Rebecca.

Megan blinked back a few unexpected tears. For all Tim's trying over the last several weeks, he'd not been able to do what the three-week-old who she was fairly certain had just soiled his diaper had accomplished—convinced her that God was completely, utterly good and had loved her into being.

24

Hunger for the Great Light

May

The car door slammed, and Alan rushed to Jamie's side. He peered at the orange brick church with its thin white steeple drawing his gaze to the cloudless blue sky. A row of ornamental pear trees in full bloom scented the air with their tangy fragrance as the sun crept toward its noonday position and rendered his suit jacket unnecessary.

Jamie had already slid out of the Miata and was tugging her skirt down. The golden tones in her red hair shone in the sunlight. He pictured it fanned across his white pillowcase this morning and smiled. Staying in bed too long had caused them to be late, but he didn't regret a minute of it. They needed time alone together, lots of it. And if he took the job he'd been offered with its two to three nights' weekly overnight travel, there'd be a lot less of it to come by.

They'd been lovers for years, but never had he felt so connected to his wife. Nothing lay between them. No unspoken hurts, no resentment, nothing held back from one another. No barriers. He didn't know enough Bible verses to fill an index card, but one of the few he did know—the one he'd heard at Chris and Rebecca's wedding and read in the hospital waiting room the night Sebastian was born—stirred his heart as they walked hand-in-hand into church. Same one he'd whispered to Jamie when he'd kissed her after nearly six long months of separation. "The two shall become one flesh."

Alan pulled open the glass door and allowed Jamie to

166

enter ahead of him. He spotted Chris and Rebecca in the first pew in front of the marble bowl where he assumed they baptized babies. A smattering of people sat scattered in a half-dozen pews, mostly family, but also a few couples Alan didn't recognize.

"Made it." Jamie sighed and squeezed his hand, tugging him up the aisle.

He caught Chris's gaze as he and Jamie slid into a pew next to Rebecca's sister, Abby, and her family. Her three children sat sandwiched between their parents, swinging their legs from their seats in the pew. Her husband Joel's hair had been shaved close to his head. Had he had the tumor surgically removed? He looked thinner than Alan remembered but as healthy as Alan had ever seen him.

Chris murmured something to Rebecca, gathered their son from her arms, and walked past their parents, bringing Sebastian to Alan.

"He was asking for you." Chris grinned as he placed the baby in Alan's arms.

Alan shifted, making sure the baby wasn't smashed so close to his chest he couldn't breathe. Sebastian's eyes were closed, his cheeks ruddy but pricked with small, white blemishes that only made him more adorable. His tiny, pink lips quirked in a momentary smile that Alan reflected back at him.

Jamie reached over him to squeeze the baby's tiny toes through his white socks. The long, white baptismal gown draped his body. A matching bonnet covered his fuzzy head, long satin ribbons lying across his chest.

A swell of emotion caught in Alan's throat, and he cleared it as he rubbed a hand across his eyes. He loved Sebastian with an intensity he'd never felt before—and the little guy wasn't even his. What would it feel like to hold a child of his own, his and Jamie's?

Jamie nudged him in the side. "You okay?" Her thin whisper made him think she loved this kid as much as he did.

"Yeah." He nodded. "I'm great."

Chris's gaze flitted between them. "So, you two, uh, everything's good?"

Jamie squeezed Alan's knee and gushed her answer. "Better than ever."

Rebecca motioned for Chris to return to the front with Sebastian as Father John emerged from the side of the altar wearing what looked to Alan like a long, white tunic and a scarf, something different than he'd worn for Chris and Rebecca's wedding. It was missing a layer or something.

Alan relaxed against the back of the pew. He wasn't quite sure yet where he stood with God, but Chris and Rebecca considered this perhaps the most important day in their son's life, a day he'd never remember. That had piqued Alan's curiosity.

Father John directed a series of questions to the parents and the godparents, a thirty-something couple he'd never met who were friends of Chris and Rebecca's and went to this church. Alan followed along as best he could, but only one thing stood out. Two sentences that nearly knocked him out of the pew.

"Sebastian," Father John said, "the Christian community welcomes you with great joy. In its name I claim you for Christ our Savior by the sign of his cross."

Whoa. He'd been claimed. Unabashed power resonated in that declaration. His nephew had been claimed for Christ. Alan couldn't help but wonder how his life might have been different had he been claimed for Christ. Or how it might be changed were it to happen now.

At the conclusion of the service, while Alan and Jamie

waited for the photo-ops to finish and everyone to gather their things, Abby loudly interrogated her children as to who had to use the potty. The preschool-aged girl seemed a likely candidate, seeing as her legs were crossed so tightly the skin on her bare calves appeared a mottled blue.

"No wonder," Abby muttered. "All that trickling water. It's a wonder *I* didn't pee my pants."

Jamie failed to hide a smile, her eyes wide. At the same time, from the front of the church, Sebastian let out an angry wail.

"Time for Sebastian's boob break." Abby again, with her kids trailing behind her heading toward the rear of the church. Joel followed.

Alan's dad took a moment to smile at his grandson and congratulate Chris and Rebecca before he cornered Father John. This wasn't a "hey, thanks for baptizing my grandkid" conversation. This was a back-and-forth with serious thought on either side. Something was going on there, though his dad had been mum.

Jamie wiggled closer to Alan, and he rested his arm on the pew behind her, smiling. He kissed her cheek, savoring every moment of being with her.

"Did you know I was baptized?" She gave him a coy look, seeming pleased she'd discovered something he hadn't known about her.

He lifted his brows. "Really? When?"

"I was about a year old. At the Evangelical Lutheran church. I didn't know until Mom mentioned it while she was staying at our place."

Jamie had been claimed for Christ too. He was starting to feel like the odd man out. Who had laid claim to him?

The small crowd thinned out. Dad and Father John shook hands and parted ways, and Mom helped Chris and Rebecca gather their things.

"But you didn't go to church, did you?"

Jamie shook her head. "My parents didn't really follow through after the baptism." She slid her hand down his forearm and interlocked her fingers with his.

Alan's gaze shifted from their hands to her face.

"Maybe it's a good place to start. Y'know, where I was baptized." Her gaze stayed glued to his face, waiting.

She must've been having feelings similar to his. This tug to dig deeper, to anchor themselves to something beyond themselves. "Lutheran, huh?"

She shrugged. "Christian. I don't know. This church is nice." She gazed at the altar, the statues, the carved images of the crucifixion hanging on the wall. "I feel like . . . like I've been invited to a banquet, but I can't even read the menu."

He chuckled. "Yeah. I guess we'll figure it out."

Mom tapped him on the shoulder as she passed, carrying the empty infant carrier. "You're coming to the restaurant, right?"

"Yeah. We're coming." Alan stood and let Jamie out of the pew.

Chris and Rebecca had stopped at the last row where a middle-aged man—Rebecca's dad? Yes, Rebecca's dad!—sat alone. Chris extended his hand, and, after a moment, Mr. Rhodes shook it, his face stoic.

A moment later, Rebecca laid the bundled baby in her dad's open arms. The man's head drooped, and his shoulders shook.

Alan squeezed Jamie's hand, trying to keep his emotions in check.

By twenty-nine, Alan Reynolds had celebrated every Christmas with Santa instead of Christ, rolled his eyes at every use of the word "miraculous," and mocked the kids who missed Sunday soccer practice for Sunday school.